DANCING IN THE DARK

CHERYL ST.JOHN

Connie—
I'm so excited to see
this series come to
life — thank you for
remembering our first
plans & being excited
with us.
Much love
Cheryl
St. John
'11

Cover & interior design by Cat & Doxie Author Services

❀ Created with Vellum

Dedicated to the memory of Barb Hunt,
who was an enthusiastic part of this series project from the very
beginning.
You and your characters live on in Spencer and in our hearts.

She'd wanted to dance, get married and have babies...all she had left was dance.
He had everything a man could want--except her forgiveness...

There had been no roadmap for life apart

Kendra Price had never wanted to be rich, but she'd wanted to be comfortable, which she was. She'd never wanted to be famous, but to live her passion to the fullest and dance, which she did. She'd wanted to marry Dusty, have babies and live happily ever after. It would never happen.

Dusty Cavanaugh has loved Kendra Price since she walked into the school cafeteria and captured a dozen boyish hearts with the sweep of her stormy gray-green gaze and the lift of her chin. College, marriage, and children had been the plan. But then Dusty made a mistake. He'd had his own baby. Without her.

CHAPTER 1

*S*team rose from the jasmine-scented water in her clawfoot tub while Kendra hung her clothing on hooks, spread the fluffy mat and set a hand towel and her phone on the stainless steel stand.

She slid down into the water, stopping at her neck, so she didn't have to fix her hair again. She might want to drive into Spencer for groceries later. The relaxing warmth felt wonderful after her drive up the mountain. Closing her eyes, she imagined the first people she'd see and how long it would take for news of her arrival to spread. It wouldn't take long for her mother or her sister to learn she was in town. News traveled fast among the regulars.

She rarely gave herself over to thinking about growing up here, but she'd never severed ties either. Each summer something drew her back. This house that her Aunt Sophie had left to her. The community. Certainly not her mother or sister. Maybe she was just being obstinate and refusing to be run off. Maybe she was a sucker for punishment.

Her bath had cooled, so she turned on warm water, and it trickled from the vintage faucet. Absently she held one foot under the stream, then the other. She rested her big toe on the side, admiring her red polish, then let the water run over it, playfully attempting to stop the stream with her toe, and getting squirted in the face for her foolishness. "Oh!"

She attempted to sit and reached for the hand towel, but her toe didn't budge.

Startled now, Kendra sat forward awkwardly and turned off the water to survey the situation. She had to bend up her knee to get a look because her toe was stuck in place. She gave a tug, and pain shot through the joint. She pulled again, harder this time, but more slowly. Her toe remained securely stuck in the faucet.

Panic set in immediately. What was she going to do? Tugging hurt too much to force it loose, and an injury to her foot would be a setback to her career. She rinsed herself off and pulled the rubber plug to let the water drain. No use turning herself into a prune.

This was a fine how-do-you-do as her Aunt Sophie would have said. Sophie would have had a good laugh over this one. Minutes ticked by. Finally Kendra admitted to herself she was going to have to call for help. Who did she know? No matter how desperate the situation, she wouldn't call on her poisonous mother or her hateful sister for help. Eying the towels on the chrome rack—so near and yet so far —she pulled the hand towel toward her and dried as best she could, then reached for her phone. Neither of them would have been any help anyway. She needed someone who could get her out of this dilemma, no matter how humiliating.

She had hired Glen Randall to take care of the monthly maintenance and evaluate the condition of the property after each rental. He had checked everything out before her return, so he knew she was in Spencer. She had no choice—it was going to have to be a man. She scrolled for his number and touched the green call arrow. The phone rang and her stomach fluttered.

"Glen here," he answered, out of breath.

"Glen, it's Kendra Price," she said. "I'm afraid I'm in an embarrassing predicament, and I need you to come out right away."

"Are you all right?" he asked.

"Yes, yes, I'm fine—"

"Kendra, I'm at Burnham Memorial right now. My wife's having a baby this afternoon."

"Oh! Well, congratulations."

"Thanks. Tell you what. I have a friend I can call. We help each other out when we have emergencies. He won't mind. I'll give him a shout right now."

"Okay." She supposed one man finding her naked with goosebumps and stuck in her tub was the same as the next. "Okay, tell him there's a key under the gnome on the back patio."

"You're not there?"

"I'm here, but—I'm stuck in the bathroom."

"I'll tell him."

"And ask him to hurry please."

"Will do."

She hung up and laid down her phone. Of all the stupid things she could have done. Why this? She gazed longingly at her robe on the hook across the room and imagined a chunky plumber in overalls showing up to find her like this. Now there'd be a new twist to the spreading news of her arrival. *Did you hear that other Price girl got stuck in her bathtub out there at her lake house?*

She picked up her phone again and opened her Facebook app. She'd occupy herself scrolling through her newsfeed. Memes of kittens and pictures of dancers didn't make her feel any more competent or less foolish, but it temporarily took her mind off the impending gossip. How long was it going to take Glen's friend to get here? A little bored and a lot impatient, she touched her camera icon and took a picture of her foot with her big toe stuck in the faucet. She looked at the image, almost deleted it, and then decided it might make a good story one day. Back to social media.

"Handyman!" Twenty-five minutes later a loud knock and the shout startled her. "Hello?"

Kendra laid down her phone and held the skimpy towel in front of her breasts, not hiding much. "I'm in the bathroom! Down the hallway and to the right!"

Boots sounded on the wood floor. "Glen Randall called me," came the shockingly familiar voice from outside the bathroom door. "Said you needed help with something?"

No. No, her mind was jumping to outrageous predicaments—more outrageous than this one. "Yes, I'm in here. Stuck in the tub unfortunately. As soon as you come in, will you please take the robe from the hook on the wall and toss it to me?"

The doorknob turned and the door swung open. "You need a robe?"

This was a predicament all right. Her heart lurched in her chest. She managed to push out a syllable. "Yes."

Six-foot-something of broad-shouldered sandy-haired male in a black T-shirt, slim-fitting jeans and workboots filled the opening. The flimsy towel shrunk even more. He had a good look before catching himself and diverting his attention.

More than embarrassment flooded her. Anger. Humiliation. She hadn't expected to have a man walk into her bathroom today, but the last person on the entire planet she'd expected to see was Dusty Cavanaugh.

The years had delivered his boyish handsomeness into dangerous maturity. She'd always envied his bronze complexion. The guy glowed after a day in the sun, while she blistered. His fair hair contrasted with his tanned skin, the ends becomingly lighter. It was short now, neatly styled, but she remembered it long and sun-bleached. "Dusty?"

"Kendra," he replied. His aquamarine blue gaze dropped to the hand towel she clutched at her breasts—and then as though remembering what she'd asked, he took a step and reached to grab her robe from its hook. "This pink thing?"

"Yes, thank you."

The bathroom was at least ten by ten. Dusty had to take three steps to hand her the robe. Politely he turned away while she fumbled with the covering and the towel. "I heard you'd inherited this place from your aunt."

"Half anyway," she said.

"So it's half yours?"

She got her robe sufficiently wrapped around herself. "No, I bought out Erica's share."

"I wondered about that."

"I made sure she didn't know the buyer was me."

"You rent it out, right? I didn't expect to see you."

"I just arrived. I'm teaching at the Holling Campus again this summer. You can turn around now."

His turned and his attention went to her toe, stuck in the faucet. "Can't say I've ever seen this before."

"I thought you were the operations manager or something at the Lodge."

"Chief engineer. All my people were busy when Glen called, so I came myself. How did you manage to do this?"

"I put my toe in and it stuck. Can you get it free?"

He knelt and leaned over the side of the tub to inspect her foot. "Does it hurt?"

"Only when I try to pull it out."

"We'll get it out. I'll try a couple of things. I'm going out to my truck. Be right back."

"I'll be here."

He raised one eyebrow in response and turned away.

Dusty opened the back of his Dodge Ram and unlocked the tool chest. For the past five—nearly six years Kendra had avoided him, except for the occasional hello. And she had every reason to keep her distance. He didn't blame her one bit. He was still angry with himself over what had happened between them. But he couldn't go back in time and change it. He didn't know if he would even if he could.

Seeing the way she looked at him carved away another piece of his soul. Never did a day pass that he didn't think of her. Never a night arrived that he didn't close his eyes as his head touched the pillow and relive the disappointment on her face when she'd learned the truth. She hadn't deserved to have her heart broken.

He placed items he needed in his metal toolbox and carried it inside, taking a more detailed look. He'd spent plenty of time at Sophie's house as a boy, remembered it well. It looked like a different place with overstuffed colorful furniture, glowing wood pieces and refinished wood floors. An enormous colorful painting of a dancer in a bell-shaped skirt hung over the familar mantle. He headed back to the bathroom with its original black and white tile. That enormous clawfoot tub was new.

"Let's try this first." He popped the lid from a jar of petroleum jelly, swiped a glob with his index finger, and rubbed it around her toe and the faucet opening. He took her toe between his thumb and forefinger and attempted to gently turn it one way and then the other.

It held fast.

Kendra gave her toe an extra tug and then yelped.

"Don't do that. We'll get it without hurting you."

She went still.

He glanced at her face, devoid of makeup, her wild

copper hair caught in a knot with strands falling around her neck and ears. Her skin was flushed, her wide eyes divulging her mistrust. The sight of her did crazy things to his heart and his head. He'd known her since he was ten years old, and she was still the most beautiful woman he'd ever set eyes on. The best thing that had ever happened to him. One of the best things anyway. He'd loved her with his whole being, wanted to make her his wife, start and end every day beside her. Her embarrassment and humiliation wounded him. Shamed him.

We'll get it without hurting you. Thoughtless words. He'd already hurt her immeasurably. Deeply. Permanently. He couldn't fix the past or take it back. "Kendra—."

"What's your next idea?"

He dropped his gaze to the pulse at her throat, where she clutched the fluffy pink robe together. She'd always shined in pink, red and orange, shades other redheads would shy away from. Not Kendra. She made a statement with her clothing choices. She was unique. Magnificent. Had been from the first time she walked into the school cafeteria and earned a dozen boyish hearts with the sweep of her stormy gray-green gaze and the lift of her delicate chin. *I know who I am, and I don't give a crap who you are.*

But she'd let down her guard and trusted *him*. Loved him. Given him her heart. He'd thrown that trust back in her face and stepped on it. And he hadn't been able to make it up to her. "Say goodbye to that antique faucet."

"I like this faucet."

"Which do you like more?"

She looked at him.

He gestured with a forefinger. "The toe or the faucet?"

She gave a resigned sigh. "Do what you have to do."

He picked up the hacksaw and glanced at her pale leg. The robe didn't cover nearly enough. Her shapely calf was visible all the way to her knee, and thankfully she'd tucked the towel underneath her, so he didn't have to avoid letting his gaze wander that direction. He experienced that thought all the way to painful pleasure and back.

Jumping up, he grabbed another towel from a rack, unfolded it and draped it over her legs, leaving only her foot showing. "Might be some metal shavings," he said by way of an explanation.

He grasped the faucet with his left hand and drew the saw across with his right.

"You won't cut into my toe," she said.

He continued to saw back and forth. He was familiar with her toes. "Unless this one has grown longer than the other, I've left plenty of leeway."

"What if we still can't get my toe out even after you've cut that off?"

"Then we can get you to the hospital, which we couldn't do with a whole bathtub attached."

"I don't want to go to the hospital."

"I'm doing my best here, Kendra."

"I know." It probably pained her to acknowledge his effort.

"Just try to relax." He sawed. It wasn't a particularly warm day, but his skin grew damp. He sensed her focus on his hands, observing the motions of his arm and shoulder. When he got up today, this was the last thing he'd planned to be doing, and she was the last person he'd expected to see. He glanced at her. Her stormy gaze skittered up to his. "My sister works at the ER at Burnham Memorial," he said to make conversation.

"I heard. Brooke, right?"

He went back to his task. "Uh huh. She took FEMA courses and learned FAA regulations. That girl put in hundreds of flight hours in order to get all her certifications for the Life Flight Team. She's done so many training hours and earned so many certifications, I can't keep up."

"You must be really proud of her."

They hadn't had a conversation this long—or this civil in years. The sound of her voice clawed another slice in his heart. "I am. Her most recent certification was so she can do solo flights with neonatal patients."

"Good for her."

There was so much more he wanted to share with her. Questions he wanted to ask. He wanted to know what she'd been doing, what her life was like in Denver. He missed her so much it was physically, painfully debilitating sometimes. He had to take a deep breath and relax his muscles. Being this close to her was like being near an electrical force.

He didn't have a right to expect anything, not even civility. So he sawed. Whenever he saw her mother, Lacey, he asked about Kendra as unobtrusively as possible. She talked about her like she and her daughter were great friends, but he suspected she hadn't seen much more of Kendra these past years than he had. He knew how Kendra felt about her mother, and the woman was still a piece of work. Bartended at the Wild Card, like she had since they'd been kids, partied as though she was a twenty-something, always had a man staying with her. Nothing had changed. "Almost finished."

He gave a final thrust and the piece of pipe broke off. Kendra lowered her foot to the bottom of the tub with a clink.

He reached for her hand. "Let's get you out."

She waved away his help. "I can do it."

Gathering her robe around her, she stood, letting the towel fall into the empty tub. I'm going to put some clothes on," she told him. "There's tea in the fridge."

He gathered his tools and left the bathroom, headed for the kitchen, where he got ice and poured two glasses of cold tea. He opened cupboards, finding them neat and orderly, until he found the sugar and sweetened his drink. He took a long refreshing swallow, and the taste brought back a memory of drinking iced tea with Kendra and Sophie in this kitchen. He turned aside, expecting to see the wooden screen door and hear the whistling *do weep do weep* of the wood ducks' screech, but the interior door was closed.

His chest ached with all the what could-have-beens crowding his heart. This wasn't how he'd planned his life—their lives. Seeing her made it painfully clear his feelings hadn't changed.

Hers had. And rightfully so.

The clink clink sound of the pipe caught his attention as Kendra hobbled to the kitchen. She entered the room, wearing bright orange-and-purple patterned exercise leggings and a little white top that showed the length of her supple arms, her slender neck and her collar bone. She still had a lithe dancer's body. She hadn't done anything to her hair, and he liked the messy unaffected look.

"I poured you a glass. No sugar."

"Thanks." She picked up her iced tea and took a sip. "Now what?"

He pointed to the jar of petroleum jelly he'd left on the table. "Now let's try this again. But first we'll ice your toe. It's probably a little swollen, and cold might help us slide off the metal."

"There's a bowl in that cupboard." She gestured.

He retrieved the large container and opened the freezer side of her refridgerator to fish for enough cubes to fill it halfway.

"Probably water, too, don't you suppose?" he asked.

"Okay."

At her nod he turned on the tap and added cold water. Behind the sink was a newly installed row of windows with a wide sill. Dusty glanced out and took in the view of Twin Owl Lake. He rarely saw it from this side anymore. He spent all his time on the Lodge side. "Is Sophie's old runabout still in the boathouse?"

"That's probably enough."

Okay. He turned and set the bowl on the floor at her feet.

She didn't look at him, instead keeping her focus on her foot. "How long?"

"At least a couple of minutes."

She stuck her toe with the piece of faucet into the cold water and grimaced. "Think that's long enough?"

"A little longer."

She had ignored his last question, so he didn't attempt to talk. He reached for his glass and took a long sip.

"Is this long enough?" she asked.

"If it's going to help, that should be enough. Let's dry it off." He handed her a dish towel from a rack and removed the bowl.

She dried her foot, and gracefully rested her calf on the table, so he could reach from the other chair.

"I'd forgotten how you could do that so easily. Lift your leg right up there."

Dusty opened the plastic jar and applied globs to her flesh inside and outside the piece of cold metal, using his finger to push the jelly as far under the edge as he could. Her skin was reddened from the frigid water. Her toes were topped with bright red nail polish.

He used the dish towel to wipe his hands, and then wrapped it around the metal piece. "Ready?"

"Do it."

He pulled, twisting at the same time.

Kendra scrunched her face, but waved at him with one hand. "Keep going."

He pressed his thumb against the end of her toe, applying

counter-pressure and worked the circle of faucet toward him. It gave way and slid off.

Kendra released a pent-up breath.

There were abrasions on the toe and it had begun to swell again. He held her foot to gently wipe it with the towel, noting scabbed spots on her other toes and reddened joints on her littlest toes. Under his fingers her calluses, more pronounced than he remembered, lined the pad on the bottom of her foot. He had the barely-resistable urge to bring her foot to his lips and kiss it. "Does it hurt?"

That was probably a foolish question to ask her.

She pulled away, tossed a clean towel on the floor and stood on it. Standing on tiptoes, she flexed her toes and arched each foot.

"Dusty," she said, sitting back down and looking directly at him.

He flinched inwardly. She was used to sore feet, and he was making a big deal of it. "Yes."

"Can this stay between us?"

"Sure." He got up and washed his hands at the sink, gathered his things and headed for the front of the house.

"Send me a bill," she called from behind him.

"I don't want anything," he replied and sailed out the front door. Now he could hear the wood ducks. The iridescent waterfowl always nested in trees in the tiny cove just to the south of Sophie's place. The sound filled him with regrets. He and Kendra had been so young, so full of hopes and dreams. Even then he'd wanted to marry her.

He packed his toolbox and climbed into his truck, turning it around and heading up the long drive to the road. He didn't look in the rearview mirror.

Kendra picked up all the towels and started a small load in the washer on the enclosed back porch. Out of habit, she used an antibiotic cream and wrapped her sore toe. She tidied the bathroom, rinsed the tub, and then poured herself a glass of wine. Carefully, she put on an old pair of canvas shoes to walk down to the shoreline. She sipped the wine. It could have been worse, she supposed. She never had visitors, and only Glen knew she was here, so if she hadn't had her phone within reach, someone might have eventually found her skeleton in the tub.

Forgetting was easier in the city. She stayed to herself as often as she liked, had dinner and drinks with friends when she wanted company, joined troupes and performed as often as she preferred. Between theater and teaching, she was doing what she'd always wanted to do. She'd trained for this life. She was good at it.

But summers drew her back to the Colorado mountains, back to the house that had been her refuge during her adolescent years. Aspen Gold Lodge owned all the land and operated the cabins on the Spencer side of the lake, but the homes and cabins on the east side had been in families for years. When her aunt had left the cabin to Kendra and her sister, Kendra had held her cards close to her chest. If Erica had known she wanted it—had known she was trying to buy it, her sister would have hiked up the price, even though she had no interest in owning the cabin.

As darkness fell, Kendra went back to the house for the bottle of Pinot Noir and sat on the bank, where water lapped and frogs chirrupped. This place was in her blood. She couldn't stay away. No, she'd have lost weight before turning into a skeleton. Her toe would have thinned out and come loose. A little tipsy now, she laughed at herself. One by one lights came on in houses and cabins, and in the distance on the opposite shore, the enormous four-story lodge lit up like a beacon. Right now people would be dancing in the ball-room, enjoying five-star cuisine on the terrace and in the dining room. Celebrities, sports figures, rich and famous—those who could afford the anonymity and luxury—had stayed at the Aspen Gold Lodge since its early days. The community of Spencer had grown and thrived with the tourist trade. Spencer was a tourist town, due to the lodge and Jakob Spencer, the patriarch who had built the hotel nearly fifty years ago, but the people who ran the shops and businesses were a tight community of families who had lived surrounded by the mountains for generations.

She'd never wanted to be rich, but she'd wanted to be comfortable, which she was. She'd never wanted to be famous, but to live her passion to the fullest and dance, which she did. And she'd wanted to marry Dusty, have babies and live happily ever after. Which would never happen.

Because Dusty'd had his own baby. Without her.

CHAPTER 2

*I*t had been twenty-eight years since Jonas Finch sat at the edge of the lake with his wife. Twenty-eight years today, actually. The world had changed dramatically since then. As had Twin Owl Lake. The bench where he sat this early morning was in fact the second replacement.

When Rebecca had died at the age of 58, he'd wished he could die too, because a life stretching out ahead of him without her had been too painful to consider. Without children, they'd been each other's world.

The spotted English setter sat comfortably at his knee, and Jonas stroked his neck. Clive was content to explore in the woods and wait right here for Jonas's return. Jonas stood, reaching for his Thermos and ignoring the pain in his hip. Normally he didn't allow himself time for maudlin thoughts, but some anniversaries couldn't be ignored. He limped down the bank to the boathouse and unlocked the padlock. In the dim interior, he unhooked the mooring line and lowered the gleaming wood 1960 Chris-Craft into the water.

He'd retired fit and healthy nine years after Rebecca's death, then moved alone to the lake house, where they'd planned to spend their golden years. His cronies at the VFW had predicted he'd find someone and marry again, but he'd known better. There would be no second Mrs. Finch.

One interminable winter he'd rebuilt the interior of the boat. He could use a smaller one. This twenty-foot beauty was too big for one person, but he couldn't let go. It held too many memories. He flipped up the throttle lever, then started the engine. After a couple of hoarse chugs, the old outboard sputtered to life, and he backed out into the sunlight.

At the sound of his motor, the pair of wood ducks that had been hiding in the tall grass led their ducklings to the bank. The lake was quiet as always this early in the morning. A hundred yards out, he surveyed the neighboring homes and cabins. Still dressed in a white T-shirt, Joe Cavanaugh sat on his dock with a cup of coffee. He'd probably had a late call and would soon be heading into his job at the sheriff's department. He and his teenage daughter were living in an Airstream while Joe constructed a cabin. Joe raised a hand in greeting.

On the property to the south of their place, Sophie Dobson's two-story home remained, still flanked by evergreens to block the view of the dam. The roof was new, though the same brick-red it had always been. One of Sophie's nieces now owned the place and rented it out to regulars, but strangely, she was always there herself during peak tourist season, June through August. In any case, Jonas appreciated the new owner's respect for the home's original beauty; even the boathouse had been refurbished and was an attractive dark green. Occasionally he noticed Sophie's aluminum runabout on the lake.

There was a fish fry at the VFW that evening. He'd probably spot some of the other old timers on the lake this morning, but he had his own secluded spot. The surrounding rivers were a mountain angler's dream. Jonas had bait and fly fished, spin casted and spent many an hour on the banks of the Big Thompson and St. Vrain, but nothing settled his soul like the lake.

The tourists crowded around the west end and under the highway thirty-five bridge, so Jonas trolled into a long narrow inlet and cut the engine. Within minutes the sounds of insects and birds resumed. Water lapped against the side of the boat. A morning on the lake was always the best way to start a day. He had supper to catch.

❧

If Piper Newport offered her one more cup of coffee or another "smidgen" of apple pie, Kendra would burst. The food was good at Pearl's Café. The establishment wasn't in Olde Town where all the tourists ate, so when she was in Spencer, Kendra brought her laptop and had lunch in town every few days. She'd already had her first run-in with the person she avoided, so that was out of the way. Today she was waiting for student enrollment notification from Front Range College about her class. She could have found another place, but she liked the atmosphere, the banter and the laughter. The volunteer firemen and sheriffs crowded around the enormous U-shaped counter for coffee and lively discussion on their breaks, and the background activity was strangely comforting. The booths with red leatherette benches were more secluded and the regulars were used to visitors and summer people, so other than friendly smiles, she was left alone to work.

The email she'd been expecting was in her inbox. Her classes were full, so her schedule was complete. She looked through the profiles of the students, planning how she would group them according to abilities and experience to effectively instruct them. The name Cavanaugh jumped out at her, and her stomach tensed. Chloe Cavanaugh. Her home address was north on the same lake road as Kendra's.

"Ready for a warmup?" Piper dangled the coffeepot over Kendra's cup.

"I've had plenty." She covered the cup with her fingers.

"Are you on Facebook?"

Kendra glanced up at the blonde wearing a red apron over jeans and white T-shirt. They'd known each other in school, enough to have a familiar history, though they'd never been close. "No, I'm planning my classes."

"No, I mean do you have a Facebook account? I could friend you."

"Oh, yes. I don't post much though." All the waitresses were friendly, but Piper went out of her way to serve Kendra and chat.

"I'll friend you. I keep tellin' Marty we should get a business account for the café, but he says there's no point. Everyone who lives within driving distance already knows we're here and knows what's on the menu. The tourists manage to find us." Marty and his wife owned and ran Pearl's Café. Kendra had never figured out who Pearl was. "It's a good way to see new faces and read about what people are doing."

Kendra gave her a smile. "That's what appeals to people, I guess."

A couple of brown-uniformed deputies entered, hanging their hats on the rack inside the door and finding spaces at the counter. The tallest made a casual check of the room, his gaze coming to rest on Kendra.

Her heart sank. It was tough not to run into a Cavanaugh in Spencer.

Joe raised a hand in greeting, and she smiled. After

placing his order, he came over and stood beside where she sat. "Looks like a working lunch." Then, "Hey, Piper."

"Hey, Sheriff." Piper carried away the carafe.

Joe looked back at Kendra. "You here for the summer?"

"I am." She should probably ask him to join her, but she didn't know him all that well anymore. "My summer classes fill up quickly."

"All the dancers want your instruction."

"Yeah, what's up with that?"

He grinned. "My daughter Chloe made sure she got on the list as soon as she saw your name."

"I saw her on my roster. She's fifteen?"

He pursed one side of his mouth. "You're twisting the knife."

She didn't know the whole story, but she knew his wife had disappeared when his daughter was young. She'd only met the woman a couple of times and, sad to think, but she'd always reminded Kendra of Erica.

"Is that Kendra Price?" The dark-haired young man who moved up beside Joe had a smile on his face. She recognized the unusual blue-violet eyes of an old classmate, now the local veterinarian. "Dr. Samuels."

"Come on. It's still Jackson. Good to see you." He gave her a friendly smile. "And this is still the best place in Spencer to grab breakfast without being trampled by tourists."

"Some things don't change," she replied. "That's kind of nice."

"I'll see you around." He headed for the gathering of men at the counter and found an unoccupied stool.

She and Joe exchanged an awkward glance. He grinned. "Make some time to see my mom. She'd like that."

"Sure," she replied. "That would be nice." He didn't mention Dusty, and she sure wasn't going to share that she'd already seen him. She might as well get it over. "How's the rest of your family?"

"Mom is good. She's in the house yet. Can't talk her into selling. Tyler's kids are in their teens too."

Tyler was his oldest brother. "I can't believe it."

"Dusty is busy. Crosby is Crosby."

His parents had adopted twin girls as well. "And your sisters?" she asked.

"You probably know Steph is the event planner at the lodge, but the latest is that Brooke is a flight nurse now."

"That's great." No one ever called his sister Stephanie.

"Nice to see you. We're neighbors, you know. Let me know if you need anything."

After he'd walked away, Piper returned and filled Kendra's water glass. "Everybody knows each other's business in Spencer," she said, slipping into the seat across from her. "Something going on there?"

"Joe?" Kendra shook her head. "I used to hang out with his brother, so I got to know the family pretty well." One Cavanaugh in her past was plenty.

"Which brother?"

"Dustin."

She raised her eyebrows in surprise. "How did I not know this?"

"I don't know." Gossip must have died down. "We kind of found each other when we were kids. He had a big loud family, and they scared me a little, but I loved everything about them. We dated off and on through high school. Then we were both in college when we got engaged. But it just didn't work out, so I got a job in Denver."

Piper studied her for a moment.

"What?"

Piper shrugged. "You never got serious about anyone else?"

"What about you? I'm telling you my story."

Piper looked away, her long blond ponytail swaying, then back. She gave a shrug. "I leave my options open."

"That's not much information."

"I'm pretty boring. Hang out with my grandpa a lot." She stood up again. "Say, there's a fish fry at the VFW tonight." Taking her order pad from the pocket of her apron, she tore off a slip. "My grandpa gets a kick out of the family going, and the fish is always good. It's just a bunch of nice old guys most of the time. Drive in and we can eat fish and chat." She looked at Kendra with a hopeful expression.

"Well...."

"Please don't say no. You can't have that much work to do that you can't come into town to eat, right? You have to eat. They serve beer on tap, but if you want something else, I can run over to Big Don's after my shift. Wine or something?"

She'd had enough wine the previous evening. Kendra really didn't have a good excuse to stay home, save the fact that there were people she didn't want to run into. Piper had been really nice to her, and she had no reason to decline. An evening with a friendly person sounded better than another night by herself. "Beer is fine."

Piper grinned. "Awesome. It starts at six. Can you meet me in the parking lot a few minutes after? I'll need a shower or I'll smell like the grill."

"Sure. How about six fifteen?"

"Perfect."

Kendra closed her laptop.

❖

The sun indicated the day had reached mid-afternoon. Jonas had released several sizable rainbow trout, since the daily limit was four, but he'd caught four the preceding day as well. Add to those the couple of hybrid cutbow and a tiger muskie now in the hold, and he headed for home. He'd bet money that muskie weighed a good eighteen pounds. The motor whined, and he cut it immediately, then raised it to get a look. A piece of net had caught in the propeller. Grabbing his knife, he cut away the offending net, finding seaweed caught and entwined with the knots. His fingers touched something hard. He poked what he guessed was a piece of root or stick with the tip of his knife, scraped away green slime and caught a prism-like reflection.

Jonas set down the knife and used his fingers to disentangle a small object, wiped it on his trouser leg and held it up to inspect. Damnedest thing ever. A ring. Diamond by the looks of it. With a thumbnail he picked algae from the prongs that held the stone and looked again. He'd find something to clean it with when he got to the house.

With the prop free, he lowered the engine and headed in. Clive greeted him with a single bark from the bank, then turned and darted for the boathouse.

"Got fish for the fry tonight," he told Clive after securing the boat and locking the doors. The dog sniffed the bucket appreciatively. He'd give Jeeter and Harm a jingle and see what they'd caught that day. Hopefully they'd have enough for a crowd.

Clive wagged his tail and followed Jonas up the worn path.

❦

Kendra had to admit she was glad she'd accepted Piper's invitation to come tonight. The fish and slaw had been excellent, and the people were friendly. She recognized several of them.

"Thanks for asking me."

Piper ran a finger over the condensation on her red plastic cup. "I see you every summer, but we've barely talked since high school." She glanced away and then back. "But you might just like it the way it is, and if you do, that's cool. I just didn't want to…I don't know…miss out on being friends if you wanted."

Not many people were as frank as Piper. Kendra admired that about her. "I stay pretty busy throughout the year, and then when I come back, I'm either teaching classes at the college, at the studio, or choosing music and planning choreography. I don't think I've really paid any attention to doing things for fun for a long time."

Several people had eaten and left, but others visited, and a group of seniors had started a game of darts. Kendra's gaze moved from one table to another and a familiar face caught her attention. The woman looked older than Kendra remembered, but it had been a long time.

Piper must have noticed her unease. "Something wrong?"

This was why she didn't go to places like this. "No, I—I just noticed someone."

She glanced over her shoulder. "Liz Cavanaugh? She's a sweetie, isn't she? We could go over and chat."

"No. No, I'd rather not."

Piper shrugged. "The break-up thing makes it uncomfortable I guess." She took a long swallow. "Shame about her husband."

"I'd heard that Sam passed away a couple years ago." Kendra waited. Would Piper reveal anything more? The possibility of running into Dusty again was always in the back of her mind. Her heart skipped a beat as she forced out a casual, "I heard Dusty had lived somewhere out west for a while."

Piper nodded. "I kind of remember that. It must have

been short lived. Look, they've got the ice cream freezers running. These old guys know how to party."

Kendra laughed.

Two white-haired gentlemen approached their table. One leaned down and gave Piper a kiss on the cheek, which she returned. "Hey, Grandpa. Mr. Finch. This is my friend, Kendra."

"What's your last name?" Piper's grandfather asked.

"Price," she answered.

Harm turned to the other gentleman. "You remember Sophie, Jonas. This is one of her nieces."

"So, you're Sophie's niece," he said, acknowledging her aunt. "We're neighbors on the lake. I was just today admirin' the work you've had done on the old place."

"Oh, yes, of course. I've seen you fishing in the morning. You knew my aunt?"

Jonas nodded. "My Rebecca and your aunt Sophie were best of friends. Neither of them ever had children of their own. I think that was something that brought them together. Rebecca and Sophie always spent a whole day pulling and chopping rhubarb. Now I tell the neighbors to come get what they want. Been a long time since I had pie like hers." His smile was wistful. "Your Aunt Sophie made the best rhubarb pie I ever ate in my life."

Everyone had loved her aunt. "I think I remember your wife."

Mr. Finch looked at her with a curious expression. He opened his mouth to say something and then closed it.

"You got something to say, Jonas?" the other man asked. "You're looking like that muskie you brought for supper."

"Kendra?" the older man said finally.

She nodded.

"That's an unusual name. Guess there couldn't be two Kendras in these parts."

"I don't think there was another Kendra the whole time I was in school."

He reached into the pocket of his pressed and pleated trousers and withdrew his hand. "My wife used to say there was no such thing as coincidence. Only the Master's plan. I pulled this from the lake today, tangled in a net that caught on my prop. Cleaned it up when I got home. Got a magnifying glass and checked it over. Name's on the inside."

He extended his hand, a ring protruding between his forefinger and thumb.

Kendra's vision blurred for a moment, and then focused on the ring he held. Fourteen karat white gold with a cluster of nine round diamonds that formed a square. The band was wide enough for an inscription. She already knew what it said. She'd read it a thousand times in the months she'd possessed it. This old man held a piece of her history...a piece of her heart.

Slowly, as if it might disappear as magically as it had appeared, she extended her hand. Jonas met her gaze, and she recognized his empathy and understanding. He knew nothing about her, but he saw right through her. He placed the ring on her palm.

She couldn't form a coherent question. "How...?"

The piece of jewelry was a sad-sweet weight. Her thoughts tumbled in chaos. Disbelief reigned. Holding this ring was the most improbable thing she could imagine. Maybe she wasn't really seeing what she thought she was seeing. Longing worked its way to the surface. She wanted this to be real. But she was afraid it might be.

And then what? Having the ring again wouldn't change anything.

She picked it up and turned the band to the side so she could look at the words of love inside.

"Whose is that?" Piper asked.

"It's mine," she replied on a breath.

"Yours?"

Kendra nodded. She'd never expected to see this ring again. She'd been hurt and angry when she'd thrown it into Twin Owl Lake. She'd never gotten over being hurt and angry, but sometimes…sometimes when she had a momentary lapse in sensibility, she'd regretted her rash action.

"How did it get in the lake in the first place?" Piper asked.

"I put it there." Kendra looked up. She'd said it matter-of-factly.

"Oh." Piper's eyebrows rose. "Well, then how did it get out of the lake?"

Jonas shrugged. "Caught it in my Evinrude this morning. Didn't seem overly strange. I've caught a lot of stuff over the years. Meeting Kendra on the very day I found it? Now that is the true miracle."

Kendra extended the ring. "You found it. Are you sure you trust that it belongs to me?"

"The look on your face when you saw it told me all I need to know."

She closed her fist around the piece of jewelry and drew back her hand.

He had the whitest hair she'd ever seen, sticking out in short unruly spikes that would make Pink jealous. His face was browned from the sun and weathered with age, but he had kind eyes and a sincere expression.

"Did you enjoy the fish?" he asked.

"Best fish I've ever had."

"Sophie left her place to you?" Jonas asked, without unlocking his gaze from hers.

"To my sister and me. I bought her out."

"Smart. The land is worth ten times what it was before Aspen Gold Lodge was on the map."

"I couldn't have been more surprised than to know she'd

left it to us. I spent a lot of time there with her, and it was…
well it was home to me."

He gave her an understanding nod, and she became aware
of the others listening. "I rent it out when I'm not here," she
told him. "Glen Randall takes care of it for me."

The sound of footsteps running toward them caught their
attention, and she was glad for the diversion. "Mr. Finch!
Jeeter! My dad's gonna take me fishing on the lake Saturday!"
The child held up three fingers. "That's this many days. I'm
gonna catch a fish as big as the ones you got today."

Kendra straightened one leg under the table to covertly
slip the piece of jewelry into her front jeans pocket and
placed her hand over the tiny bump, feeling it safely nestled
there.

"I'll bet you will," Mr. Finch told the fair-haired little
fellow. "You're growin' up to be quite a fisherman."

"I got a fishing pole, too." His bright blue eyes were wide
with excitement, and the color gave her a start. "A really long
pole. An' we're gonna dig some worms."

"I might see you out on the lake," Jonas told him.

"I'll wave," the boy said in all seriousness.

Jonas chuckled.

"Ian?" Liz Cavanaugh joined them and touched the child
on the shoulder. She glanced at the two gentlemen and then
at Piper and Kendra. "He's a slippery one."

"I was talkin' with the fishermens," Ian said.

Kendra met Liz's eyes, and the woman offered her a
gentle smile. Kendra had spent many hours at her home, in
the kitchen, at the table with their family, had imagined
herself one day being a part of that. She held no hard feelings
for Liz, and she doubted Liz held any toward her. Why
would she? It had been Dusty who had brought their plans
and her world crashing down.

"Hello, Kendra. You're looking as lovely as ever."

She and this woman shared something. "Thank you. It's good to see you."

"I guess you met my grandson. This is Ian." The boy attached himself to her jean-clad leg and looked over at Kendra.

Kendra got up from her chair and knelt in front of him. "It's nice to meet you. I'm Kendra."

"Use your manners, Ian," Liz urged softly.

Suddenly shy, Ian extended his hand and she enfolded his small fingers in her grasp. "Nice to meet you too," he said bashfully.

Kendra glanced up at Liz.

"Ian is Dusty's son."

Of course, he was. The world narrowed down to this room, this moment, to the child before her, and the soft narrow hand in hers. *Dusty's son.* Her chest ached with the weight of loss. Betrayal manifested in one beautiful, blameless little person. He'd changed her life. Her future. His conception had shattered her hopes and dreams and stolen the family she'd wanted. Through no fault of his, Ian was the reason she'd moved to Denver, the reason she avoided Spencer, the reason she stayed to herself. The reason all her hopes and dreams were under lock and key, and she had to face every day with new focus and purpose.

She swallowed hard.

She'd recognized the child immediately. His eyes were disturbingly familiar, along with his arched brows and square chin. The delicate curve of his upper lip was nothing like his father's however, and yet painfully recognizable. She wanted to close her eyes against the stabbing shard of grief this child caused, but she couldn't. He was as blameless as she.

Dusty's son. The child that should have been hers.

CHAPTER 3

*D*usty found a parking spot in the nearly-full lot. His mom had taken Ian for a couple of hours when he'd gotten an emergency call earlier this evening. His position as chief engineer over the cabin and cottage rentals afforded him evenings with his son, but occasionally his men were unavailable and Dusty had to take calls. When that happened, his mom or one of his sisters were always happy to entertain his smart, happy five-year old. Ian would be starting school in the fall, and Dusty was having trouble adjusting to the fact that his baby was already old enough for Kindergarten.

The mouth-watering smell of deep-fried fish met him as he entered the building. Several people greeted him. He found his mom at her usual table, sitting with her friends. Ian was cheerfully drawing on his Boogie board. He glanced up. "Dad!

Ian climbed over his undaunted grandmother to get to Dusty.

"I told you I wouldn't be long."

"Did you fix everyone's problems?" Ian asked.

"Your old dad's good at fixing everyone's problems," he answered with a grin.

"Get yourself something to eat," his mother told him.

He helped himself to a couple of pieces of fish and the coleslaw. Jeeter brought him a red plastic cup of foamy beer.

The old Rockola started up and Elvis sang *Don't be Cruel*.

"Loydell must've brought herself a bag of quarters," his mom's younger friend, Lila Quinn said with a grin. The postmaster, Loydell Hendershot loved Elvis and would play his songs all night long if no one else beat her to putting their quarters in the slot.

"I love this song," Rowena Irwin answered. She was in her sixties, widowed, and the mother of two sons. "Let's go find partners and dance."

Lila laughed and raised questioning eyebrows at Liz.

"You two go. I'll stay here with my fellas."

The two women left the table.

"Kendra is here," Liz told Dusty.

"Yeah, I saw her yesterday," he replied. *Boy, had he seen her.* The alluring images had been in his head all day.

"You did? Well, I meant she's *here*."

"Oh." He glanced up and took in the people at the other tables and on the dance floor.

"At the table under the stained-glass lamp," she said. "With Piper and Jackson Samuels."

He spotted her. Jackson reached for Kendra's hand, and she joined him on the dancefloor as the song ended and *Let Me Be Your Teddy Bear* played. She filled out a pair of jeans like no one else. She wore a silver top with a little orange jacket and flat-heeled orange shoes. Her shiny copper hair bounced as she danced. Jackson was a little older than he and Kendra, but she might find his boyish good looks appealing. The thought made him feel sick, even though logic told him the two were merely friendly acquaintances and this was a casual night at the VFW. Rowena Irwin was dancing with Old Jeeter for heaven's sake, and no sane person could fabricate something sexual out of that.

"She met Ian," his mother said.

He glanced at his mom and set down the crispy piece of fish he'd picked up. "How did that go?"

"He's Ian. What's not to love?"

Dusty watched his son doodle on the LCD writing tablet. Right. Ian yawned and rubbed his eye. What was not to love? Except the fact that Dusty had fathered this child without her.

"She's here for the summer," Liz said.

He nodded.

"That means you'll be running into her. I'm not going to avoid her. I love that girl." As though she'd immediately realized what she'd said, her gaze shot back to her son's.

"I know, Ma. It's okay. I'll be good with it. I saw her yesterday actually. Glen's wife had their baby, and he called me to take a call on the east side of the lake. I saw the address and wasn't sure if it was a renter or Kendra. She sure wasn't expecting me."

"What was it?"

"What was what?"

"The baby. Did they have a boy or a girl?"

He shook his head. "I don't know." He turned his attention back to Kendra with the vet on the dance floor. "Do you think Jack is good looking?"

"Jack's very nice looking." She glanced in the direction he'd been staring. "You could probably get in a dance before Ian gets too tired."

"She barely talks to me."

"Dancing is conversation without talking."

He took a long drink of his beer and his mom handed him a plastic container of breath mints. He rolled his eyes, but he took a couple and reached to pat Ian's head. "I'll be right back."

She saw him coming toward them, and Kendra's eyes widened. She looked at Jack and then away.

"Hey, Jack," Dusty greeted him.

"Dusty."

"Mind if I cut in?"

Jack shook his head and left the floor just as the song changed again. The strains of *Are You Lonesome Tonight?* flowed around them.

'Are you lonesome tonight, do you miss me tonight? Are you sorry we drifted apart?'

"What are you doing?" Kendra asked in a low voice.

She was still the prettiest woman he'd ever seen. Her stunning red hair and fair skin took his breath away and made his heart beat a little faster. He remembered her dewy fresh face and the ivory skin she'd tried her best to conceal the day before. "It's a small town. We're going to run into each other." He raised his hands waist level.

Her gaze moved to those around them and back to him self-consciously before she stepped closer. Dusty rested a hand at her waist and took her other hand. She smelled incredibly good. He wanted to bury his face in her hair and travel back to a time when this had been so natural...so right. They'd always fit together perfectly. There had been a time when the fact that she'd become a professional dancer had intimidated him, but she'd laughed and told him this wasn't professional dancing and he wasn't a dance partner or a student. He was the man she loved and her life partner.

He *had been* the man she once loved.

Surprisingly, she relaxed and fell into step. *'Is your heart filed with pain? Shall I come back again?'*

There had been many nights like this, evenings at high school dances and prom, even a few nights at the lake, a CD playing from the truck while they danced under the stars. Nothing had changed. Everything had changed. His every breath reminded him he was alive, and as long as he was alive, there was hope. He was going to give Loydell another roll of quarters to thank her for this moment. "Mom said you met Ian."

"I guess it was inevitable."

"Five years," he added.

She looked up at him, her smoky eyes filled with hopeless questions. "He's beautiful, Dusty."

Her admission must have cost her, but it killed him. His throat filled with a wave of emotion, and he clenched his jaw to keep the feelings from jettisoning from his soul. The song ended, another started, but he barely recognized it. They moved in unison while he gathered his composure. He had so much to say, but he couldn't form the words.

Kendra's head felt light. She'd only had one beer, and it wasn't particularly warm in here, so Dusty's closeness was the only explanation. She hated feeling vulnerable.

She looked aside to turn her focus on the couples near them and stop the crazy beating of her heart.

"Kendra, I've tried to apologize. I know you haven't wanted to hear it, and I respect that. But when you're ready to hear my apology, will you let me know?"

She let herself look at him. He had the best face—a straight nose, beautifully-shaped lips, eyes so blue she lost herself in their depths, and enviable thick lashes. A familiar dear face that stole her heart and her common sense. He wore that five o'clock shadow with so much sex appeal, she considered what it would feel like to brush her cheek against his…to kiss those lips.

She hated him. She wanted him. She wished she'd never met him. She wished nothing had ever had to change, but it all had. She didn't want to hear him say he was sorry. She was glad he was sorry. "What's the point? Your apology can't change anything. Except to make *you* feel better."

"I understand, Kendra. I do. I can't take anything back. I can't change what happened. Nothing happened the way I wanted it to, but I have Ian now, and I can't regret him."

She pulled from his loose embrace and they stood apart as the songs changed. "I'm not talking about this with you. You have your life now. I have mine. I don't know what you want from me, but whatever it is I can't give it. I can't possibly give it, Dusty. Have enough respect for me to accept that."

It was obvious he wanted to say more. His eyes revealed his regret, but he said nothing. She wasn't going to let him ruin her summer or chase her away. She had as much right to be here as he did, and she was tired of walking the tightrope that was Spencer, Colorado and Dusty's home territory. "We're in the same town. We're going to see each other. But we don't have to dance and act like nothing ever happened."

"That's not what I'm doing. I admit what happened, Kendra."

Her eyes widened and she squared her shoulders. "And you're okay with it."

He shook his head. "No. Not like that. I live with this regret."

The ring he'd given her, along with pledges of love and forever burned in her front pocket. She should take the offending reminder out and give it to him. She got a little nauseated at the idea of parting with the ring Jonas had found in the lake after five long years.

"Kendra—"

She fished in her pocket and pulled out the engagement ring. "Do you remember what it says inside this ring?"

"What...?" His expression showed his complete surprise. "How did you get that?"

"Seems Jonas Finch caught it in the lake this morning."

"That's impossible."

"What's inscribed on the band, Dusty?"

"Can we take this outside where we can talk?"

"You can't say anything that will change the situation."

He worked his mouth in a movement of frustration. "You're right." He lifted both hands and took a step back. "I can't change the past."

"You should have this." She extended her hand and attempted to give him the ring.

He left his hands in the air. "I gave it to you. I don't want it."

"You could sell it," she pointed out.

He put his hands on his hips. "So could you."

Did anyone have as much forgiveness in their heart as it would take to excuse him and move on? Just looking at his grim expression pained her. It should have given her satisfaction, but somehow knowing he lived with regret hurt worse. Maybe she just had to be here in Spencer, seeing him, seeing his son to get past it. Like ripping off the band-aid and letting air get to the wound. There was no healing without pain, no acceptance without grief.

She tucked the ring back into her jean's pocket. "You're right. We have to learn to coexist. You're someone I knew from a long time ago. This is now." Everyone else sure seemed to have moved on as though nothing had happened. She couldn't feel more out of sync, any more like an outsider. But she'd always been on the outside looking in, and she'd done just fine. Maybe she did need friends in Spencer, because she sure didn't have family. But this man wouldn't be one of them.

She shook her head. "We can't be friends. Everyone makes choices. This is mine. If hell freezes over and I want to hear your apology, I'll let you know."

Without another word, she turned and walked away.

❖

Dusty watched her go, his heart hammering in distress. She said something to Piper, picked up an orange handbag and made her way around a gathering of men on her way to the door. The door opened and closed, and she was gone.

Someone else had commandeered the Rockola. Freddie Mercury was singing *Crazy Little Thing Called Love* and Dusty stood on the edge of the crowded dance floor.

"Want to dance?" Lila Quinn asked with a friendly smile.

He glanced at her. "Thanks, but…you know, I'd better get Ian home to bed."

"Sure, see you later."

He nodded and headed for the table where his mother and son sat. "Let's go home, buddy."

"Looks like it didn't go too well," Liz said.

"It was okay until I mentioned apologizing. She doesn't want to hear it."

"I'm sorry, honey." She got up and gave him a hug, then bent to give her grandson a hug and a kiss on the cheek. "Why don't you fellas come over for supper tomorrow?"

"That sounds good." Dusty brushed her cheek with a kiss and took Ian's hand. Minutes later his son was buckled in and they were headed for home.

"Kendra's pretty, isn't she, Daddy?" his son said from the back seat of the truck.

"Yes, she is."

"Are you friends with her?"

"I was once."

"Kinda like me'n Oliver. We were friends. He put my backpack in the toilet at school, remember? Now he's not my friend."

"Something like that."

"Did she break something of yours?" Ian asked. "Or say something mean?"

"No. She's a kind person."

"Miss McIntyre made Oliver say sorry."

"Did you forgive him?"

"I said I did."

"Sometimes people do dumb things, and afterwards they're sorry," Dusty told him.

"I just don't want to be his friend anymore. Caden is nice to me, and he's my friend now. We make forts together an' his mom makes good snacks."

"Snacks are important," Dusty agreed.

"Uh huh." Ian yawned loudly. "I'm gonna close my eyes for a minute."

The child was asleep within seconds, so Dusty took the road that led southeast around the lake to clear his mind. He passed cabins and houses set back from the road and others disguised by trees. He spotted his brother Joe's Airstream glowing in the moonlight through a stand of conifers.

He turned off his headlights and slowed to a stop across the road from Sophie's house. Kendra's house now. He took in the familiar wide front porch and the twin dormers with charming paned windows. Last time he'd driven this road in daylight he'd noticed the new red roof that looked just like Aunt Sophie's original. There was dim light from one of the upstairs dormers now, but the road was too far from the house to make out any shadows or forms. He knew the floor-plan well enough to know there was a bedroom at the front of the house on the main floor with a window facing the porch, and two more upstairs.

If she bathed in the main floor bathroom, it was likely she slept there too. He wondered only momentarily what she might be doing upstairs. She probably had a studio room. He pictured her stretching, dancing…maybe wearing clothing like she'd worn the day before. Five years ago, he'd thought nothing could hurt as much as her throwing that ring in the lake, turning her back on him, and leaving Spencer. He'd been wrong. A lot of things hurt equally as much. Her expression tonight, her holding that ring out to him like a dagger, her refusing his apology—the pain was still fresh, the self-inflicted wounds as deep as ever.

Sitting here was pretty stalker-ish, and he had Ian with him, so he put the truck in gear and moved on, switching the lights back on. His brother was the sheriff, but he still didn't want to be seen watching Kendra's house like some kind of wacko.

His life stayed on an even keel most of the time. He kept it that way for his sanity and Ian's well-being. He always hoped something would happen to restore what had once been. News of her arrival, his brief glimpses of her, reports of Kendra every summer now all caused an upheaval in his emotions and narrowed his thoughts back to how it had once been between them, what had happened and the part he'd played. This was worse than other summers. Seeing her up close, talking to her, dancing with her, smelling her….

He had to get a grip on himself. He'd do everything he could to earn her forgiveness, but in the end—if he had to—he would let her go. He couldn't die trying because he had someone depending on him. Listening to Aerosmith, he headed for home.

❦

The bright-faced young students set their bags along the wall and removed their shoes. A couple of them stretched and another secured her hair. Kendra recognized Chloe Cavanaugh's shiny mahogany hair tethered in a neat braid.

She looked like Joe, who had darker hair and eyes than Dusty.

Kendra picked up her roster. "Good morning. I'm Kendra Price. Welcome to contemporary dance class. I'm looking forward to working with each of you this summer. I'll check off your names first, and then I'd like to see what you can do. I'll give you a fifteen-minute warm up, and afterward you'll take turns dancing to the music I've chosen. You won't be graded on anything. This is only so I'll know where to start. I like to teach each person individually at their level."

She started with the nearest girl and got her name. She asked the students how long they'd been dancing, where they had trained, their favorite styles. When she reached Chloe, the girl gave her a bright smile. Chloe wore her straight reddish-brown hair in a braid with a slim beaded headband. She was delicate and vulnerable looking, so unlike her strapping father and uncles in manner and appearance. Kendra studied her a moment, taking in her brown eyes and translucent complexion, finding the resemblance to her mother and the shape of her mouth like Liz's.

"It's great to see you, Chloe. You were dancing when you were just a little bitty thing. I remember you put on a program for the family one Sunday after dinner."

Chloe covered her face with one hand, but she was smiling when she removed it. "Oh, that's embarrassing. I didn't remember. And you were there?"

Kendra laughed. "Yes, I used to come to a lot of Sunday dinners at your grandma's. I thought you were pretty good for five years old. Where have you been studying?"

"Dobson Studio. Lynette Kinsey was my instructor when I was little, and now Tina Albright, her daughter is my teacher."

"Sounds as though several of you studied at Dobson." Kendra observed the line of girls who were listening. "Sophie

Dobson was my aunt. She and Lynette were my first instructors."

She glanced back at Chloe. Joe's wife had left them when Chloe was a baby. Kendra would bet anything Liz had sewn beads and sequins until her fingers bled and had attended plenty of recitals for her granddaughter. She gave the girl a smile. She wouldn't have become a dancer without her aunt's help and support.

Chloe's bright expression revealed she was plainly in awe of Kendra. "But then you studied at Cleo Madison Roberts Academy in Denver and have been in her dance theater. I saw pictures of the CMR troupe performing for the president."

Kendra nodded. "You've done your homework on me."

"I tried to get into this class last summer, too, but I was still too young."

"We're going to talk about that." She moved along until she'd spoken to each young dancer, and then asked the girls to join her seated on the floor. "There's a reason I teach students your age and not children. I want to educate about more than steps and posture and routines. I want to teach you about your bodies and about the changes and growth you're going through right now. Have any of you had a problem with self-confidence or noticed a difference in your abilities, so much that you've sometimes wondered if you've lost your talent?" She looked into their faces. "Be honest. It's nothing to be ashamed of. We all go through it. Anyone?"

Becca, a fair-skinned student with ruddy cheeks tentatively raised her hand. Another nodded and raised hers. Before long, most of them had their hands in the air.

"We're going to spend some time each session talking, because it's so important that you understand how your physical changes, your increased body mass and your fluctuating hormones impact your coordination and balance. As your height and weight increase, muscle strength can be affected because your nervous system is working overtime to catch up."

The girls listened with rapt attention and a few glanced at each other.

"Did you know the long bones in your arms and legs grow faster than your torso?" Kendra asked.

The girls shook their heads.

"They do. So, the proportions of your body—actual skeletal changes—are decreasing your flexibility. Because of that you can even be more susceptible to injury, especially in areas like your knees, where strong tendons are attached."

Several sets of eyebrows went up.

"Yeah. Have you ever felt like you weren't performing at your previous skill level? Or maybe like you're not improving?"

Half a dozen girls nodded their heads.

"We're going to talk about nutrition, about modifying your technical training, about limiting high impact activities, about medical help and the emotional issues involved in this period of your instruction. Most importantly, I want each one of you to understand that this period, which could last another year, is temporary."

"That's a relief," Abby said on an expelled breath. "I was thinking maybe I couldn't dance anymore."

Kendra shook her head. "This is an important time in your life. You're still dancing, so that means you're serious and passionate. You're deciding on colleges and committing to career paths. Choices you make now can affect your professional development and your health for the rest of your lives. If you let me, I am going to help you through this season—and hopefully what I share will improve your confidence and skills for the long-term."

Tabitha, a long-limbed dark-skinned girl had tears on her

face. She swiped them away and gave Kendra a tremulous smile. "How come no one told us this stuff?"

"I didn't know it until I had gone through it the hard way," Kendra said with a shrug. "But then I did a lot of research. I'm making it my mission to educate young women and instructors. A lot of girls fall out at this age, thinking the challenge has become too difficult or that they just don't have what it takes. But I learned differently, so I'm teaching you. You will teach others."

"Do boys go through this too?" Chloe asked.

"You bet they do. And there are a lot fewer males who make it as far as you have. Their bodies are doing crazy things, too, and it's embarrassing for guys to have their voices change and their bodies change, plus be clumsy on top of it all."

Abby giggled and others joined her.

The ice was broken. "All right. I'll start music, and you have fifteen to warm up and stretch. Then we'll see what you can do with choreography."

The girls were more at ease as they found places around the room to go through their warmups and practice steps. Kendra watched them with fond appreciation. This was part of the reason she came back to Spencer each summer. Encouraging young dancers was as much of a high as giving a magnificent performance. She felt fortunate to be able to do both. This part of her life was rewarding, uncompromised.

That's why she gave it her everything. Dance never let her down.

❦

"My dad said you used to be Uncle Dusty's girlfriend." Chloe

Cavanaugh had finished warming up and carried her water bottle to where Kendra stood.

Kendra looked up from checking the notes on her tablet. "A long time ago. I've known your family since I was a kid."

"My age?"

"Younger. I was probably nine or ten when Dusty and I became friends. Growing up I spent a lot of time at your grandparent's house. Your grandma was good to me. She always invited me to supper or offered whatever she had on hand. I probably ate with them more than I ate at home."

"Your mom wasn't a good cook?"

Lacey Price wasn't a good anything, except maybe bartender. She sure hadn't been a good mom or even a decent role model. "She was gone a lot."

"My mom left us when I was little," Chloe told her.

She had her dad's dark hair and hazel eyes, but her features were delicate, and her eyes tipped up at the outer corners. She had a sweet, vulnerable appearance. "I'm sorry."

"Did you know her?"

"I saw her around and at Cavanaugh gatherings, but I didn't really know her."

"I have a few pictures."

"You're pretty like her."

Chloe gave her a hesitant smile. "Thanks. So, did you want to marry Uncle Dusty?"

"I thought I did." Kendra raised her voice to the rest of the dancers. "I'm going to show you the choreography I want you to learn this week. I'll dance it first, and then I'll go over each sequence."

Chloe grinned and took her spot. "I can't wait. Your bio says you performed with Tobin Dance America in Chicago and at the JFK Center in Washington. What was that like?"

"A lot of work. No sleep. Bruises and aches and sore feet."

She looked at the girls' faces. "And amazing experiences I will always cherish."

"Why did you quit?" Abby asked.

"Young dancers are added all the time. The others fight for their positions, and it isn't always pretty. It's a lot of travel and a lot of rehearsals. I'm glad I did it, but I love to teach almost more than I love to perform. And I enjoy coming up with choreography. I didn't quit entirely. I'm simply very selective about what I chose to do. I have plans for a new direction."

Kendra had warmed up previously, so she did a few preliminary stretches and changed the music. It still remained to be seen if she'd picked the right music and steps for this group. This was *Speechless* by Dan and Shay. She took her position as the song began and moved into the music. She never thought about anything except the phases, transitions and rhythm when she danced. It was a feeling of freedom and accomplishment she never tired of.

When the piece grew to a close, Chloe clapped enthusiastically. "Can you teach us to do that?"

Her enthusiasm exhilarated Kendra. Chloe was the student every instructor yearned for. Eager, gifted, disciplined. With deep satisfaction and confidence, she replied, "I can."

After watching the girls and running them through several sequences to learn their strengths, she was confident she had a couple of outstanding dancers in this group.

Her summer was going to be better than she'd anticipated.

❦

Two hours later, she and Chloe exited the music and arts building on the Holling Campus, bags slung over their shoulders, and carrying water bottles. They'd both showered and dried their hair before leaving. "Need a ride?" Kendra asked.

Chloe pointed to the parking lot. "My dad's here."

Joe climbed out of a black SUV and stood behind the door, his forearms resting on the top. He wore sunglasses, his sheriff's uniform and hat. He raised a hand in greeting.

Kendra waved back. "You did great, Chloe. I'm excited to have you as a student."

"I had to beg my dad for this class. He thinks I do okay at the studio."

"I'll talk to him," she promised. "You're already gifted, but you're going to grow and improve. We're going to be taking videos for instruction, and at the end of the summer, I'll show you the difference. We'll show him too."

Chloe gave her a grateful smile before running toward her dad.

Kendra walked toward her car to note someone leaning against it. After her initial surprise, she recognized the person wearing a Guinness beer tank top and skinny jeans with sandals. Her long wavy hair was light from her cheeks to the ends with eight inches of dark at the roots. The look was in fashion, but on Erica it reminded Kendra of someone not keeping up their dye job.

"Is the Cavanaugh girl one of your students?" her sister asked.

"Hello, Erica."

CHAPTER 4

*H*er sister pushed away from the side of Kendra's car and faced her. "I figured if I didn't come find you, we'd never see each other."

Kendra fished in her bag for her sunglasses and slipped them on. "I never know if you're in Spencer or if you're elsewhere. Keeping track of you was never easy. And we don't have much to talk about."

"I've been here a couple of months now."

This time. Probably after a relationship with yet another deadbeat had soured.

"I'm in a nice place over by Brook Park Drive. It's brick apartments. They just refinished the wood floors." She had a few lines around her mouth that Kendra didn't remember, but she'd always had beautifully-shaped lips with a distinctive delicate bow in the upper one.

The sight pressed a weight on Kendra's chest. "Sounds nice."

"And yes, I'm working. At Whispering Pines. I got a key and everything."

Kendra couldn't remember if that was a restaurant or a

bar, but she didn't care. She unlocked her car with her remote and tossed her bag in the back.

"Have you seen Mom yet?"

"No."

"How long are you going to stay mad at me?"

Kendra closed the rear door. Even Erica's voice irritated her. "How long do you suppose I'll live? Another sixty years or so? That ought to cover it."

"I'm your sister."

Kendra opened the driver's door, then slowly turned and faced Erica. "You might have thought about that six years ago."

"You're such a bitch to hold a grudge this long."

"Yes, Erica, I'm such a bitch. Do you even hear yourself? Acting like all you did was wear my shirt and spill something on it. Like I'm bent out of shape because you took twenty dollars from my purse—which you also did a hundred times, by the way. As though somehow I'm the one at fault here."

"You two were broken up."

"We argued sometimes, like people do, but we didn't break up until after I found out what had happened. I loved him. You knew I loved him. You knew I wanted to marry him."

"I had too much to drink—"

"Well, the apple doesn't fall far from the tree." She didn't want to say these things. She didn't want to discuss anything with Erica. She extended both hands toward the sky and then dropped them to her sides. "You know. I don't want to hear your excuses—which by the way are not excuses. Your lack of self-control and anything-goes lifestyle do not excuse screwing my fiancé. There is no excuse."

"It wasn't like he loved me or anything. You could've married him anyway."

"Not when you had his baby, Erica. Not when you

betrayed me in the worst way possible and didn't even regret your behavior." She raked the other woman with a disdainful glance. "You never even apologized. Do you know that?"

"I'm sorry! Is that what you want to hear? I'm sorry."

"What do you care what I want?" Kendra asked without raising her voice. "When did you ever care about my feelings? Don't come around my work anymore. Don't come to the house. Don't show up anywhere I am this summer. We don't have anything to say to each other. Why do I have to repeat this every year?"

She got in her car and only then noticed the note on her windshield. Getting out one last time, she peeled the paper out from under the wiper blade and again closed the door.

'Give me a call. I have something for you.' A phone number and Dusty's name had been scrawled in blue ink.

She crumpled the note, but couldn't bring herself to litter, so she stuffed the paper into the well inside her car door that she reserved for used tissues and gas receipts.

Erica gave her the finger before turning and getting into a small blue car. Ignoring her, Kendra backed out and left the parking lot without another look. She could feel the rising heat and tension in her body from the encounter with her sister. She had to hold herself back from stomping on the gas pedal. She took a deep breath to calm herself.

Sometimes Erica was gone when she arrived for the summer, and other years she was here. Why she ever thought Kendra would want to see her was beyond rational thinking. Erica was the reason life had blown up in Kendra's face. It had taken two, of course, but her sister fully admitted they'd both had too much to drink, and she didn't remember clearly what had happened. However, she hadn't admitted her deceitfulness until Dusty had told Kendra about the pregnancy.

Occasionally she stopped to ask herself why she came

back each summer. She didn't need to expose herself to this. She could perform and travel. But then she reminded herself of the classes like the one she'd just begun. Chloe came to mind…and all those girls with looks of relief and incredulity over learning their bodies weren't betraying them. All the crap had to be worth that. She could deal with her sister and Dusty, and she'd deal with the past for those moments of pure joy in accomplishment. She was making a difference in lives. She had a goal and a purpose. And she had the lake house.

She drove north to the Valley View Mall and parked in front of the Natural Grocers, a market with a large organic produce selection. Finding a playlist, she selected a song and sat for the few minutes it took to compose herself before going inside. After purchasing groceries, she stopped to put gas in her car before going home.

Starting a playlist at home, she made herself a quick meal and ate at the kitchen table. Afterward she'd cleaned up and done the dishes when the old-fashioned brass bell on the door grated its hoarse chime.

A tall figure was visible through the filmy glass panes on the door. She moved the curtain aside and got a sinking feeling in her stomach. *Really? Right now?* She opened the door and faced Dusty through the screen.

"Did you get my note?"

"I got it. What do you want?"

"I have something for you."

"I don't want anything."

"You'll want this." He opened the brown paper sack he held and revealed a vintage faucet similar to the one that had been destroyed. He raised his eyebrows and lifted one side of his mouth. "Yeah?"

She wanted to shut the front door and not handle another uncomfortable encounter today, but she'd been looking at that sawed-off faucet for two days, and the one he held was a nice replacement. Really nice. She stepped back and gestured with a sweep of her arm. "Come in."

He turned and picked up his toolbox and opened the screen door with the same hand that held the bag. "Won't take me long."

She gestured with an open palm in the direction of the hall. "You know the way."

He strode past her, and she caught a whiff of his clean scent, like line-dried laundry and sun-warmed skin. She ignored the buzz along her spine.

"What's this song?" he asked.

She'd forgotten the playlist that was her constant background. "It's called *Valerie*."

"I couldn't place it at first, but it's Amy Winehouse, yeah? I like the horns in the live version."

With raised eyebrows, she watched him disappear into the hallway, then went back to the kitchen, cleaned the sink and wiped the already spotless counters. *Can't Get You Out of My Head* came on with its contagious la-la-las. She had her workout music on shuffle. She waited for the song to end, so it didn't sound obvious she'd cut it mid-track, and then switched to a classical selection. She might as well clean the kitchen floor.

"Come see," Dusty called later from the bathroom.

She found him putting his tools away. He straightened and looked to her for a reaction.

She neared the tub and discovered the replacement faucet looked as though it had been there forever. It was in better shape, in fact, still shiny. "It's perfect. Thank you."

"My pleasure."

Apparently, he'd brought his own rags to clean up, because there was no mess anywhere. She glanced at him. "What do I owe you?"

"This one's on me."

"No, I can't let you pay for that faucet. It couldn't have been easy to find."

"I'd like to give it to you, Kendra." His gaze moved to her pink robe on the hook and then to his toolbox. His blue eyes darkened perceptibly. He bent and picked up the case. His shoulders under his cotton T-shirt were broader and more muscled than she remembered.

She didn't want to owe him. His gesture made her uncomfortable. "I insist. It was my own foolishness that necessitated cutting the faucet." She paused a moment. "I don't want a gift from you."

He raised his chin a fraction and set his mouth in a line before digging long fingers into the right front pocket of his jeans and fishing out a folded paper. Holding it between two fingers, he extended his hand.

She took the paper and unfolded it. The receipt was from a salvage company in another county, and the amount of sale was eighty-five dollars plus tax. "I'll write you a check."

He followed her along the hall, but stood near the front door while she got her checkbook. She paused. "What about labor?"

He angled his head. "It won't do any good to argue with you, will it?"

"Not a bit."

"I get forty-five dollars an hour."

He'd searched for this faucet and probably driven to pick it up as well. She added two hour's wages, signed the check and tore it from the pad. "Thank you. It was thoughtful of you to find that and bring it out."

He took the check. "No problem."

"I mean it. Thank you."

He gave a nod. Their gazes locked. Behind her, the

soothing music contrasted with the tumultuous energy vibrating between them. "You're welcome."

He opened the screen door, closed it behind him and walked across the porch, taking the stairs two at a time. *I hate it when you leave, but I love to watch you go.* That backside and those long legs in a pair of jeans could stop hearts. An elusive memory came into focus. He was fourteen or fifteen, tall and lanky, his shoulder-length hair bleached from the sun as he walked toward his dad's old Mercury, turning back with a grin to wave at her. The image was so clear that she felt the same peculiar sense of loss and longing she experienced every time he'd left to go home. But today Dusty didn't turn around...or grin...or wave. He put his toolbox in his truck, climbed in, and turned the vehicle around in the drive.

She watched the truck until it reached the road and stared after it long after the vehicle had disappeared behind the trees. He had never married. He'd remained a single father for five years. What did that mean? He was probably liked by everyone in Spencer, and he was a catch. Surely there were women who'd gone after him. The guy oozed sexy. She'd have thought he'd want someone to help him raise Ian.

He couldn't have held out, thinking there was still hope for the two of them. She'd made that crystal clear. She had no illusion that he couldn't find someone to fill that place. But the fact remained, he was still unmarried.

He'd made a mistake with Erica. Everyone made mistakes. But this one cost her everything. It cost him everything too, but it had given him a son. Erica had turned over that baby so fast, the ink hadn't been dried on the court documents by the time Dusty changed the first diaper. Kendra had no misconception that Dusty cared even remotely for Erica. Or that there'd ever been more than that one encounter between them. But that moment had changed everything.

Sometimes she wished she'd been able to move past his indiscretion. She'd tried. This wasn't the life she'd planned. She didn't want to be bitter or unforgiving, but here she was, watching him go. She missed what-could-have-been so badly that she lived with an empty ache. But she had dance. She had determination. She had self-respect.

What she didn't have was the man she'd wanted with her whole heart.

❦

Kendra'd had Sophie's boat inspected and the engine tuned before her return. She hadn't yet taken it out on the lake, but this seemed like a good evening for a ride on the water. She dressed in long lightweight pants and sprayed herself with mosquito repellant before heading down to the boathouse. The high-pitched call of a wood duck got her attention, and she spotted the beautifully plumed male, its head black with iridescent green shimmer and a distinctive white patterning on its body, perched on a dead limb that hung out over the water. Several females swam gracefully nearby.

"Sorry to disturb you," she said to the duck. "I'll be out of here in a few minutes and you can go back to courting."

The boathouse was painted bright green as it always had been. The sturdy structure had weathered many a Colorado winter. She unlocked the side door and, once inside, rolled open the wide door to the lake that protected the interior.

After turning on the power for the lift pump, she adjusted the lever and watched the boat slowly lower into the water. She removed the guide ropes, climbed in, started the engine and slowly motored out of the boathouse onto the lake. Once free of the shore, she increased speed and enjoyed the breeze in her hair. Steering the runabout was as freeing as dancing. Aunt Sophie had taught her how to do both. Sometimes she felt the woman's presence on the wind, in the tall grasses that swayed along the banks, in the sparkle of the sun on the water. She could still hear her gentle encouragement, feel her hands on her waist, see the light of pride in her eyes, feel the love of the woman who had been her teacher, her friend, her confidante…her mother in all respects except biological.

She knew the lake like the back of her hand, knew where the submerged trees were and how to avoid them. Stopping, she cut the engine, closed her eyes and listened as nature became audible. Insects buzzed above the water. Water lapped against the side of the boat. In the distance a dog barked. Jonas's old hound, no doubt after a rabbit or a raccoon.

Kendra let the peace and tranquility of the lake heal her frenetic mind and sooth her doubts as it always had. This felt right. She was where she was supposed to be. These experiences were why she tuned out everything else in order to be here.

She watched as the sun lowered in the sky above the Aspen Gold Lodge. She didn't trust herself alone on the water after dark, so she enjoyed a few more brief minutes and then started the engine and headed home.

❧

Dusty's cell phone vibrated, and he glanced at it. "I need to take this. Excuse me."

"Go ahead." Jakob Spencer waved him off. Their quarterly budget meeting was important, but Dusty's position required him to handle emergencies. The other executive officers around the conference table gave him nods.

He tapped his phone screen before he got to the door. "Cavanaugh."

"We have a dishwasher flooding the kitchen on the mezzanine. I can't get a hold of Brewster."

"Unplug it from the wall. I'll be right there." He shot to the elevator and waited impatiently, trying Ted Brewster's phone and pager unsuccessfully. Thankfully the elevator was empty, and he left a stern message for the appliance tech.

When he arrived at the kitchen of the Gold Room, the lodge's most exclusive restaurant, Wilson Young, the chef was in a state. "I still have all the herbs to chop for tonight's filet of bison. The pan-roasted pheasant is on the menu. I need my kitchen! I can't work in this—this monsoon!"

"We'll move you to the Mediterranean Room to prepare your dishes, Chef Wilson. I'll have everything you need taken there. Give me a list. I'll call in another assistant, just to run for things you might need." Dusty glanced at two kitchen helpers, nervously standing by. They were obviously staying out of Chef Young's way. "Get carts and start stacking every-thing Chef Wilson tells you to get."

Dusty grabbed his phone and called the operations desk. "I need help cleaning up water in the Gold Room. Drop what you're doing and get a crew. If Brewster doesn't return my call in the next five minutes, I'm calling Landmark Services."

Dusty commandeered one of the rolling carts and started loading boxes of meat.

"We'll have your kitchen dry and that dishwasher running by dinner time," he assured the anxious chef.

By mid-afternoon the dishwasher was working, the Gold Room kitchen was restored to order and Wilson Young barked commands to his staff as usual. Dusty hadn't eaten since morning, but he returned to the Mediterranean Room's kitchen and appeased the staff and cooks who'd been put out by the emergency, as well as by Wilson commandeering their space. "Thank you to everyone for making the best of the situation."

"You would do the same for our kitchen," the assistant chef said. "Cecilia has lunch ready for you on the balcony. Take a few minutes to sit and enjoy."

He hadn't eaten since six that morning. "I appreciate it. Thank you."

After enjoying albacore tuna and tomato wedges on a bed of lettuce, accompanied by crusty bread, Cecelia brought a slice of pumpkin cheesecake and a cup of coffee. "I won't want to go back to work," he said with a grin.

An attractive brunette at a nearby table gave him a friendly smile. A lot of single guests stayed at the lodge. Single or without their spouses, anyway. Rigid screening and privacy restrictions allowed guests to stay without fear of being seen by media. He'd run into celebrities and public figures numerous times, and occasionally answered a bogus call to a cabin from a female who only wanted male companionship.

A couple of times he'd given in to temptation, and who could blame him? No one had been hurt, but the encounters left him feeling empty. Too many people knew him and his family for him to provoke gossip or face the need to explain himself. It was easier to focus on Ian and his job and avoid complications.

No one else could ever match up to Kendra anyway. No one else could fill the place in his heart that longed for her.

He finished his coffee and nodded a polite dismissal to the brunette before leaving the balcony through the kitchen and heading back to work.

❦

"Why don't you come for Sunday dinner?"

That's what Liz Cavanaugh had asked when Kendra had run into her at Valley View Natural Grocers. Kendra had inspected the red bell peppers and zucchini with intense interest.

Dusty's mother had been insistent. And exceptionally kind, as always. "I've missed you."

Now she waited at the end of her drive in a floral calf-length cotton dress, holding a basket of rhubarb jam tarts. She canned rhubarb every summer, as her aunt had done, and from a thick stack of yellowed recipe cards with Sophie's spidery scrawl listing ingredients and sketchy directions, she'd made almost all of the recipes during her summers at the cabin.

Joe's truck approached, Chloe leaning out the passenger window waving, her mahogany hair a charming tangle of curls in the warm breeze. The truck slowed to a stop and Chloe flung open the door. "Miss Price! I was so happy when my dad told me we were picking you up. Come on. Get in."

Kendra set the basket on the seat, and Joe passed it into the back. After climbing into the cab, shutting the door, and fastening her seatbelt, she told the girl, "You can call me Kendra when we're not in class."

Chloe grinned ear to ear. "Cool."

Kendra had agreed to this visit, but even after Liz's reassurances, she had plenty of reservations.

"Oh, I don't know," she'd told the woman. "I have some painting to do."

"You have to eat. It's not that long of a drive. Joe could even pick you up. Chloe's already been singing your praises."

"She's a joy to have in my class. She has so much potential."

"You can convince Joe of that. He thinks she'll ignore her studies."

"I did both. She can too. She's bright, and she's determined."

"You're the perfect example. Joe needs to see that. And Brooke and Steph would love to see you."

Kendra gave her an uncertain look.

"You've already run into Dusty, so that's out of the way. You can't say no."

She should. "All right. Yes."

"Good! I'll see you Sunday, noonish."

Kendra nodded and gave her a weak smile. "Noonish."

And that's how she'd come to be riding with two members of the Cavanaugh family, on her way to have Sunday dinner with a dozen or two more. Okay, when she thought about it like that, she and Dusty would barely have to see each other in that crowd, let alone talk.

Once they arrived, Liz pulled her into the enormous sun-filled kitchen, where aromatic smells teased her nostrils and half a dozen female voices stopped mid-sentence. For several seconds the tick of a kitchen timer was the only sound.

"Kendra!"

"She's here!"

"Mom said you were coming!"

The females broke the silence at once, enveloping her, giving her hugs and making her feel as welcome as they had as a girl. Her nose stung and tears formed in her eyes. Rapidly, she blinked away the emotion.

"Let her breathe," Liz chastened. She handed Kendra a cutting board and a paring knife. "Here you go, darlin'. Slice and chop the cucumbers for a salad, won't you? They've been washed."

Kendra eyed the formidable pile of vegetables and set to work.

Chloe brought a huge bowl and followed her grandmother's directions for the dressing, and together the two of them made a beautiful salad, adding halved cherry tomatoes, avocados and chopped radishes.

"Brooke, you're a flight nurse now?" Kendra asked the lovely young woman with startling blue eyes and jet-black hair pulled back into a thick ponytail. She'd been a pretty child, but she was stunning now.

"She has so many letters behind her name, she could play Scrabble with them," Stephanie said with a laugh. "I'm not kidding you either. Tell her all of your certifications, Brooke."

Brooke's cheeks turned pink at the attention. "Oh, each company has its own requirements in order to fly as the solo nurse onboard a life flight. So, in addition to my ICU experience at Burnham Memorial, I had to have certain certifications like ACLS, NALS, PALS, BLS, TNCC, ITLS and CFRN."

"They all stand for something important, but we have no idea what," Steph said with a laugh, obviously proud of her sister and enjoying teasing her. Stephanie had black hair, too, but she wore it in a shoulder-length straight cut. She resembled her twin, but they were fraternal. Her eyes were brown, and she was taller. They'd been adopted as toddlers, and the Cavanaugh family had grafted them into their hearts as though they'd been born to them.

Kendra had often thought how fortunate the twins were. Even though they had difficult beginnings, they'd found the open, loving arms of parents who adored them. They had each other, and they had their older siblings. Hand-me-downs probably didn't feel so bad when the person wearing them felt special and loved, not like no one took the effort to buy them clothing, or cared how they looked, or spent their paycheck paying off their bar tab.

Looking at Brooke and Steph now, smiling and tossing a carrot back and forth, Kendra wasn't envious. It wasn't bad to want the same things other people had. It was human nature to compare and contrast. The past was the past, however, so she locked away her musings immediately and wiped the island counter.

"Joe said he saw a lot of workmen at her house after your Aunt Sophie passed on." Colette, a petite blonde with a big laugh, was married to Liz's oldest son, Tyler.

Kendra remembered her as an affectionate mother to her two small children, and Liz's right-hand helper on days like this.

"I kept the original integrity of the house and the period, but I had the floors refinished, painted all the rooms, laid kitchen tile. And I bought new appliances. I created a studio in the largest upstairs bedroom, so it has a new floor, mirrors, and handrails along a wall."

"It sounds amazing," Colette told her. "Whenever one of us saw news of your appearances, we shared it with each other, so we've followed your career. I'm very proud of you, and I know the others are too."

Kendra couldn't think of anything to say for a minute. She caught her lower lip with her teeth and blinked. "That's so nice of you. All of you."

Liz tucked an arm around Kendra's shoulders. "You're still part of our family, honey. We didn't know how to keep in touch with you, but we cared all along."

Kendra nodded. "I know. I left in a hurry and didn't want to be found, so I changed my number and kept my new one unlisted. I did read all of your Christmas cards—and the notes you sent—in the summer when I came to the lake."

"That's the only address we had for you," Colette said with a grin. "Christmas wishes in July is a little strange, though."

Chuckles erupted, lifting the mood.

"Kyle and Avery must be teenagers now," Kendra said to Colette.

"Kyle is fifteen. He plays drums in the band. Avery is thirteen and is a star soccer player. She also won a trophy at the state music festival for piano this year."

Footsteps sounded on the kitchen tile as the fair-haired five-year old darted into the kitchen. "Grandma!"

Liz dropped her hot mitts to lean down and give her grandson an enveloping hug.

"Hello, Ian!" came greetings from the others.

He turned and grinned at his aunts. His gaze landed on Kendra. "You danced with Daddy at the BFW."

Children were observant and honest, and Ian's quick association caught her by surprise. "I did. I met you there, and we had fish for supper."

"Daddy took me fishin' yesterday and I caught two fishes!" He held up the appropriate number of fingers.

And kids were easily distracted, thank goodness. "Two? Wow? That's terrific. Did you help clean them?"

He nodded enthusiastically. "It was dithgusting. But then we cooked 'em in a big pan on the fire and ate 'em."

She grinned. He was adorable. So smart and the way he spoke enchanted her. "I'll bet they were good."

"Yes, ma'am. They were de-*licious*." He rubbed his tummy.

Even his aunts laughed, and Liz gave him a kiss on his head. "*You're* delicious, Ian."

He made a comical grimace and rolled his eyes. "Nah. I'm a little boy."

"Ian, would you like to wash your hands and help me set the tables?" Steph hung a dish towel and drew a stool over to the double sink set into the enormous island.

He clambered up and extended his palms for the liquid soap Steph pumped into his palms. "I won't break nothing, Grandma."

"I'm sure you'll be very careful. Kendra will help."

Sam and Liz had added onto the back of their home, extending the kitchen and creating an enormous eating area with two walls of windows and a wall of storage for dishes. Steph opened cabinets and showed Kendra how to drape the tables with white muslin cloths and where the plates and flatware was stored.

"White tablecloths?" Kendra asked.

"Mom is hella smart. White is bleachable."

Kendra nodded. "Right."

Voices reached them from the front of the house.

"Don't be shocked if Crosby has brought a girl you don't recognize," Steph said softly. "We won't either. There's a new one every couple of weeks. Personally, I think it's time a twenty-six-year-old at least made a commitment to a career, if not a partner. He's a year older than Brooke and I."

"I guess it takes some people longer to find their paths," she replied.

"He's not looking for a path," Steph answered. "He's lived here since college, and when Dad died, we all felt better knowing he was here with Mom. Now, though, I don't know who takes care of who. She's perfectly capable of being on her own, but I am glad she's not entirely alone."

Ian chattered about his friends at daycare, and Kendra turned her attention to listening, while helping him place the forks and spoons in the right spots. Before long, Liz and Colette carried out the food.

"Go call Daddy and the others," Liz told her grandson, and he ran off.

Kendra rubbed her palms on the skirt of her cotton dress. So far, the afternoon had been lovely, but now…now she was going to see Dusty—in this setting where in the past they had been a couple.

CHAPTER 5

*K*endra glanced at the table nervously. The family undoubtedly had their usual places to sit. Liz wouldn't expect her to sit beside him like before, would she?

The older woman picked up on her hesitation. "Sit here beside me, Kendra. Tyler sits in his father's place now, but we're flexible."

Kendra took the seat offered, thankful for Liz's intuition, and breathed a bigger sigh of relief when Brooke sat on her other side.

Dusty led his elderly grandmother to the opposite side of the dining room and held a chair for her at the end of the table. She sat, patted Dusty's hand between both of hers, and gave him a wink. "Thank you, Dustin."

Ian scrambled up on a chair beside her. "Hi, Grandma C."

The older woman gave the little boy a broad smile. Dusty took a seat between Ian and Chloe.

Kendra hadn't seen Naomi Cavanaugh for many years, and she had aged considerably in that time. Her hair was dark, but obviously dyed, and she wore a long-sleeved white summer dress with black beads around her neck.

"Grandma," said Joe, who took the seat next to Naomi. "Do you remember Kendra Price? She used to be here for Sunday dinners all the time when we were kids."

The older woman peered at her, and Kendra wasn't sure she remembered, but Naomi nodded and gave her a smile. She was related to the Spencers through Jakob, the patriarch who had owned the lodge for generations--which meant all of the Cavanaughs were shirttail relation to the Spencers. In the 1900s Aspen Gold Lodge had given birth to Spencer, Colorado and consequently brought prosperity to an entire region. She made a mental note to ask about the family connection later.

From the head of the table, Joe held serving bowls for his grandmother while she served herself.

Seated to his left, Crosby had indeed brought a young lady. The family treated her graciously, but it was apparently obvious to everyone except Shay Garland that she was one in a string of Sunday dinner companions. Kendra felt a pang of sympathy for her. These Cavanaughs got under a person's skin and being a part of this family was a heady allure. Kendra herself felt as though she'd come home.

As the meal progressed, she couldn't avoid noticing Dusty. He helped Ian cut his food and occasionally picked dropped bites out of the child's lap. Once she saw him lean and whisper something in Ian's ear. The boy ate a piece of steamed broccoli and looked to his dad for approval. Dusty acknowledged with a smile and a nod.

Dusty was a father. He encouraged his son to eat vegetables. A piece of chicken stuck in Kendra's throat, and she took a drink of water. Dusty was doing all the things she'd imagined a father did—the things she'd seen Sam Cavanaugh do. The things she'd seen Tyler do when Kyle and Avery were little.

Ian was loved and accepted and an important part of this amazing and wonderful family. He had aunts and uncles and cousins, a grandmother and even a great-grandmother. And he was quite obviously loved and adored by each of them. He felt here as she had always felt at her Aunt Sophie's. Wanted. Welcome. Accepted.

The reality pleased her…and it confused her at the same time.

Her emotions didn't need another spin around the block of muddled thoughts. This reunion had been inevitable. She returned to Spencer every summer, knowing these people lived here, knowing she'd eventually come face to face with Dusty. With Dusty's child. Maybe she'd wanted this—wanted to see him for herself. Wanted to force herself to acknowledge the facts. Well, she was confronting them now.

Ian looked like his father. He fit into this family. But as kind and generous as they were, she was still an outsider. She should have been used to it by now, but the sting was fresh today.

This family knew how to make quick work of clean-up and dishes. Dusty, Joe and Tyler scraped and stacked all the plates and carried them to the kitchen. The twins handled leftovers, and then Liz and Colette loaded the dishwasher and hand-washed what didn't fit. Kendra dried and stacked bowls and pans, and Avery put them away. Chloe and Crosby's girlfriend had gone outside with Ian and the brothers to set up games.

"Tyler will get out the ice cream freezers, and later we'll have homemade ice cream," Liz told Kendra. "Let's leave the rest."

Kyle came for the bags of trash and carried them out.

"Thank you, Kiley-boy," Liz said and gave him a peck on the cheek.

"You're welcome, Grams."

These people didn't mess around with Sunday afternoon festivities. There were two inclined boards with holes cut in them and painted scores assigned for points. Steph explained the game was called cornhole. Colette divided everyone into teams and the teams took turns throwing beanbags at the holes. Playing was more fun than Kendra had expected, and the good-natured competition kept her laughing.

Each time she looked at Dusty, she experienced different feelings than when she'd interacted with Ian. She didn't much like herself for how she felt. Kendra didn't want to forgive him. But she had to. For her own health and peace of mind. In order to move on.

She'd believed she was moving on. She'd moved on all the way to Denver. She'd challenged herself and developed a career. She could go right now and find a spot in any dance company she chose. She had the freedom to achieve the things she wouldn't have accomplished if she'd married Dusty, settled down in Spencer, and had a couple of kids.

But that hadn't been moving on. She'd been running. Evading. She'd always known that truth, but it was more obvious than ever today.

How did a person forgive? Was there a method—a rule? A book? Probably a hundred. She wished she could talk to Aunt Sophie. She closed her eyes and tried to imagine the advice her aunt would have for her. Sophie had been kind and generous, but practical and no nonsense. She'd never wasted a second of her life feeling sorry for herself. Is that what she'd been doing? Feeling sorry for herself? She hadn't thought so.

Maybe she was just angry. Righteously angry. She had a

right to feel that. She had a right to her feelings, whatever they were. They were real to her.

Someone bumped into her from the back, and she turned as Dusty steadied her. "Sorry."

"My fault," she replied. "I was daydreaming."

Her arms felt slender and toned under Dusty's gentle hold. She smelled like blooming lilacs on a summer breeze, and he released her quickly, though she hadn't pulled away. "Daydreaming is dangerous in this crowd."

"I remember that now."

He loved her voice. Steph handed Kendra a stack of bean-bags, and she stood with her toes on the chalk line in the grass and aimed the first one at the board. He wasn't watching the bags land; he was watching her. She must have scored big points, because her team cheered.

He'd believed this was where she should have been all along, right here, part of his family. But truthfully, he'd always had reservations about holding her back. Maybe he'd unconsciously sabotaged their relationship because he hadn't wanted to stand in the way of her career. He'd gone to a conference in Philadelphia once, scheduled while her troupe was performing at the Kimmel Center on Broad Street. He'd purchased tickets ahead of time, because admittedly, he followed her career.

It seemed foolish now, but he'd taken great care with his shirt and tie, wearing his best suit, getting his hair to look just so. As though she was going to see him, when he would be only one in an ocean of faces. As though it mattered how he looked when he saw her. He'd actually been nervous to see her perform.

She'd been stunning. He'd watched with his heart in his throat, amazed, enthralled, in love. Sometimes while he fell asleep at night, he thought of her dancing. Sometimes he dreamed of it. And occasionally in those dreams, all the others faded away and she did see him—she came to him. Sometimes they were lying in the tall grass near her boat dock, and he was holding her in his arms. In other dreams they sat on the porch swing he'd hung when he'd bought the house that he and Ian lived in. She leaned against his chest and the scent of her hair, the softness of her body resting against his was so real, he got tears in his eyes when he woke alone.

She was perfect. Beautiful, talented, smart…. But she couldn't stand the sight of him. He didn't blame her. He'd had to move on. He'd taken responsibility for his child, and he wasn't sorry about that. Ian brought him joy and filled his life immeasurably.

Being Ian's dad felt like being rich when another person was struggling to make ends meet. Like having an abundance of food when another was going hungry. Ian was his biologically, legally, in every way, but still—today—Dusty struggled with feeling like a thief. Being Ian's father meant he'd taken something from Kendra.

He couldn't change anything. And he wouldn't if he could. He loved his son with a fierce protectiveness. His life was right here in Spencer. His world revolved around his boy, his family, his job. Regrets were a waste of time.

Kendra was watching with a tender smile as Avery handed Ian beanbags and the boy tossed them underhanded toward the holes. Ian's cousin coached him to take his time and cheered him on. Dusty worked to interpret the expression on Kendra's face, not seeing resentment or anger… seeing instead something akin to yearning.

He held a fist over his heart, wondering how he would feel if she'd had a child that wasn't his. How he would feel someday when that undoubtedly happened. All those experiences would be uniquely hers and he'd have no part in them. He'd be an observer.

Beneath his fist, his heart forgot to skip a beat.

That was how she felt. They'd planned a life together. There'd been no roadmap for life apart. Each of them was navigating their separate destination without GPS. He understood.

Dusty reached for her arm again, this time to gain her attention. His fingers rested on her warm skin only a moment before she turned and lifted her smoky gray gaze to his, a question in their depths. Words stalled in his chest.

"It's your turn, Dusty," Joe called, but right then Joe's phone rang, and he took it out of his pocket and answered it.

"I'm staying," Chloe said, with a roll of her eyes. "Aunt Colette, can I go home with you guys?"

"What's she talking about?" Kendra asked.

"When Joe's phone rings on Sunday, it means he has to answer a call," Dusty replied.

"Oh, sure. He's the sheriff."

"Chloe," Joe began.

"I'm going home with Avery. Aunt Colette said it was okay."

He nodded, then glanced at Kendra.

"I'll run Kendra home," Dusty said from beside her. He didn't look at her.

"Great." Joe gave his mother and grandmother each a peck on the cheek and headed for his vehicle.

Dusty checked on the ice cream freezers with Tyler and, with Ian at his side, went to the kitchen for a couple stacks of plastic bowls and spoons.

Folding chairs had been lined up around a firepit, and as the sun went down and the air cooled, the twins built a fire, and the family migrated to sit near it. Ian and Avery carried bowls of ice cream until everyone had one. Kendra sat between Chloe and Avery and appeared amused by the teenagers' conversation.

"It almost feels like she's never been gone, doesn't it?" his mother observed from beside Dusty.

"Almost."

"Have the two of you talked?" she asked. "I mean actually talked…about what happened and how you both feel about it?"

He shook his head. A minute later, he added, "Jonas Finch found her ring in the lake."

"Her *engagement* ring? But how?"

He shook his head. "Found it cleaning a bunch of seaweed off his prop."

"How is that even possible?"

"I don't know. But he gave it to her, and she tried to give it back to me. It was the same ring."

She glanced over at him. "You didn't take it."

"I wouldn't take it the day she threw it in the lake. I don't want it now."

"You love her."

"Never stopped."

"She belongs here. She belongs with you."

He shook his head. "She has a career. She's an amazing dancer, Mom. She could be performing anywhere right now. I mean it. She's that good."

"But she isn't performing elsewhere. She's in Spencer. She's *here*."

"She likes to teach at Holling. She loves our family."

"I have eyes, Dustin. She loves *you*."

Kendra glanced their way just then, caught him looking at her, and raised her chin in the merest acknowledgement. "Did Joe really have a call?" Dusty asked.

"You give me far too much credit. Of course, he did." His mother got up and gathered bowls from those who had finished eating.

The sun had slipped behind the mountains, but it wasn't

yet dark. Dusty checked his watch and called Ian. "Time to go!"

Ian gave all his aunts, uncles Tyler and Crosby, and all of his cousins hugs before heading for the truck. Kendra had finished helping clear away dishes and chairs and said her goodbyes. She carried her empty basket.

"Those were delicious," he told her, nodding to the empty container.

"Aunt Sophie's recipe." She opened the passenger door and climbed up to the seat, arranging her dress over her legs.

Ian was already in the backseat. "We have one quick stop to make, and then we'll head for your place."

She nodded. "Okay."

Ian spoke from behind them. "Grams is gonna give me Grampa's fishing hat and one of his fishing poles. I'm gonna catch even more fishes then! We hafta dig some big fat worms, huh, Dad?"

"You bet we will," Dusty replied, used to the constant chatter.

"Someday maybe we can get a boat and fish like Jonas and Harm."

"Maybe we can."

"Can we get a boat, Dad?"

"Boats take a lot of work, and you have to have a place to store 'em," he answered. "There are the rentals on the west side, though. We could do that like we did last time."

"What's a rental?"

"You pay to use a boat for a few hours."

"Oh. That's how we got the boat b'fore, huh?" Silence, as though the boy was thinking that over.

"I have a boat you can use."

Dusty looked over at Kendra then. She was watching the street ahead.

"You have a boat?" Ian squeaked from the back seat. "Dad,

Kendra has a boat an' she says we can take it fishin' in the lake! This is the best!"

"That's generous of you," Dusty said, carefully. The runabout had been her aunt's and obviously meant a lot to her. "Are you sure?"

"I only use it a couple of times a week. You might as well enjoy it."

"Thank you."

"Can we take it fishin' next Saturday?" Ian asked.

"You certainly may," she replied. "If it's okay with your dad," she added quickly.

"It's good with me." Dusty took a route through Spencer, around Brook Park, and drove west on Forest Lake Drive, past the high school and the ball fields. Kendra sat up straighter, and he sensed her tension.

"Where are we going?" she asked.

"Dropping Ian off to spend a few hours with his other grandmother. She doesn't work on Sunday evenings."

Kendra's stomach had plummeted as soon as she'd seen the road they were taking, the familiar landmarks and signs. *Timberline Outfitters, eleven miles.* Matt Chandler's place. *The Aspen Gold Lodge, thirteen miles.*

"His other grandmother's?" she managed to say around a knot in her throat.

Dusty nodded.

"He goes to her house?"

"Yes."

"Grandma Lacey has Legos and little cars and stuff. We play with 'em," Ian said.

Kendra felt as though she was going to throw up. *Ian spent time with Lacey Price.* "I'm not getting out of this truck."

"No, that's fine. I'll just run Ian in and be right back. He stays a few hours and I go get him later."

Her entire body tensed with dread at being here and with

concern for the child. Dusty's child, she reminded herself.
She had no say in what he did. She pursed her lips and sat
rigidly as they passed along the tree-lined street she hadn't
seen in years and parked at the end of the driveway.

Her senses were numb, but she made herself look at the
house. It had been painted white, and the overgrown spiraea
bushes she remembered around the front steps and porch
were no longer there. Cement planter boxes sat on either
side of the porch steps, but they were empty.

Dusty opened his door, and then the rear door, and
helped Ian to the ground. Taking him by the hand, he led him
toward the house. The front door opened, and Lacey Price
came out to meet them, waving a little, smiling. She wore
slim jeans and a tank top, and her blond hair was pulled back
on both sides, revealing dangling earrings. She looked the
same, but older. Still thin, still wearing clothes appropriate
for someone twenty years younger.

She didn't look toward the truck, only leaned forward to
wrap an arm around Ian's shoulder. She straightened and
looked at Dusty as he spoke to her, nodded and opened the
door to lead the boy into the house. Dusty went inside with
them and didn't come back out for a few minutes. Kendra
watched the door close and took a deep breath to quell the
uneasiness in her stomach. Okay, at least he was in there
checking out the place.

The door opened again, and he emerged. Dusty glanced
at her as he returned and climbed into the driver's seat. He'd
left the engine running, so he backed the truck onto the
street.

She tried to bite back her words, but restraint was hopeless. "I can't believe you leave him there."

"She asked to see him when he was a baby, and we tried a
few ways of making it happen. When he was small, she came
to see him at our place. He likes her."

"He's five and a half. He'd like Ted Bundy."

"She's his grandmother, not a serial killer. I wouldn't leave him there if I didn't believe he's safe. We have rules. The are no men there while he visits. No drinking. I go in and look around. It's clean. He's safe."

They rode in silence until reaching the highway that lead to her side of the lake.

"Does *she* see him?"

He knew who she meant. Her sister. "No. She has no interest." He slowed around a curve. "I can't even imagine how hard this is for you."

"No, you can't."

"Lacey goes out of her way to make time to spend with him. She buys things for him to play with."

She couldn't even conceive of it. Nothing in her experience gave her a mental image of her mother taking time to show interest in a child. Lacey'd never had time for her own daughters, never made time. Kendra didn't believe the woman could just change and now be happy to have a grandkid around.

Kendra considered her vehement reaction and reasoned with herself. Was she jealous because Lacey had never shown the least interest in her, but bought Legos and played with Erica's child?

She caught her runaway thoughts and dialed them back. Kendra had never learned when to cut and run. She just kept coming back for more. Her anger dissipated, and she leaned back against the seat, tired now. Exhausted from this day. She, who could train and repetitively execute minute choreography for hours on end until her feet bled, who could do two performances a day for a week, she was exhausted after Sunday dinner and a few games. It was the emotional toll; she recognized that. It was this man. His family. His son. She wanted to lie down and be enveloped by the nothingness of sleep. She closed her eyes.

And behind her eyelids immediately saw Ian with her mother. She covered her face with her hands.

"Are you all right?"

She lowered her hands and opened her eyes, the lush bristlecone pines along the side of the road a blur of shadowed greens now that darkness was falling. "I'm fine."

"I don't think you're fine."

"You don't know me."

"I think I do."

"Well, you don't."

He turned into her drive and slowed to a stop. For the first time, the sight of the home that had always been her refuge failed to buoy her spirits.

Dusty didn't turn off the engine, but he asked, "Can we talk?"

Finally, she turned and looked at him. Took a good long look. He shared handsomeness with the other Cavanaugh men, but he had fair hair while the rest were dark-haired. His skin tanned easily, however, she remembered from their summers at the lake. She'd become burnt even with sunscreen and a long-sleeved shirt, while he'd unfairly tanned. He was not quite as tall as Joe, but still reached six foot in stocking feet. He was leaner than his older two brothers, but with corded muscle in all the right places.

He had feathery pale lines at the corners of his eyes, and a small scar near his eyebrow she didn't remember. His lips were nicely shaped, full, and his cheeks held creases that deepened when he smiled. He wasn't smiling now.

Thinking about reaching over and tracing those creases, touching that scar with a fingertip created a flutter in her chest. They had once been that familiar with each other.

They'd been comfortable with closeness, intimacy, private smiles…dreams.

She wanted to feel like that again. She wanted to love like that again. She craved a gentle caress…being held….

He was waiting for an answer.

She held onto the basket in her lap. "We've talked enough for today."

"Soon then?" he asked.

"I need a little space."

"Okay." He turned off the engine, got out of the truck and came around to help her down. Always a gentleman.

He reached for her hand, and she took his, feeling the calluses on his palms, the warmth of his fingers, the current of awareness that darted up her spine.

"I'm glad you came today. My mom enjoyed having you. Everyone did."

She nodded. "It must be difficult for her without your dad."

"It is. But she's strong. She hasn't missed a beat."

She let a moment pass. "I'm sorry I didn't come to his funeral."

"It's okay. You were working. You know how those things are, there are so many people you can't even talk to everyone and then later barely remember who was there."

She nodded. She should have come anyway. She couldn't change the fact that she hadn't now. "Goodnight."

""Night, Kendra."

She felt his gaze as she walked to her door and let herself in. She didn't turn around, didn't stop until she was inside and had shut the door behind her. Before turning on a light, she moved to the window and peered out from behind a curtain.

He had walked back and opened the driver's door, and

now stood in place with the dome light on. Waiting until he saw lights on in the house.

She reached for a wall switch that flipped on the lamps in the living room. She peeked again; he got in, turned the truck in the drive and headed away from the house.

Kendra switched off the light. She went out and stood on her porch to listen as the sound of his engine disappeared. Slowly night sounds replaced the rumble.

Would she ever be strong enough to forgive?

CHAPTER 6

*E*arly Monday morning Kendra worked on the choreography she'd be teaching her class that afternoon. Before taking a shower, she pulled rhubarb and cut weeds around the enormous rows that grew every year. She washed, chopped and stacked bags in the freezer, then made three pies, a rhubarb crisp and the flakey pastries that were her favorites. After cleaning up, she took a quick shower, packed her bag for dance later, and headed to the boathouse.

She had two pies safely stored in containers as she motored out onto the lake. Behind her the wood ducks called out their high-pitched 'eeep eeeps' that always sounded like a question. Overhead a few puffy white clouds painted the broad sky in its summer glory. She headed northwest and stopped, turned off the engine, and removed her straw hat. She could have driven, Jonas's place was short of a mile by car, but she'd needed this time on the lake. The sun felt good on her face. Closing her eyes, she allowed the peaceful sounds of water lapping the hull and a single gull overhead to clear her mind.

Dusty trusted Lacey with his son. At least for a few hours on Sundays. Well, Kendra was alive, so it wasn't as though the woman's neglect had ended in total disaster. Depending on one's idea of disaster. Neglect and emotional abuse were every bit as hurtful. Kendra captured her thinking. It wasn't like the woman was responsible for Ian or had any authority in his vulnerable little life. Thank goodness. What must Liz think of those Sunday afternoon visits? Her adoration for the child was plain.

After several minutes of drifting on the current, she once again started the engine and headed for Jonas's place. Minutes later, she docked her runabout, picked up her containers and climbed out of the rocking vessel onto the wooden ramp.

The English Spaniel whose bark she'd heard occasionally echo across the water loped to greet her, tail wagging. Kendra reached out with her palm turned downward and let the animal sniff. Satisfied, he ducked his head under her hand for a pet. She grinned. "You're a friendly fellow."

It would be nice to have a pet, but she moved back and forth between here and Denver, and she had an apartment there. Others in her building had dogs, but she often took trips, so all the machinations necessary to make being a pet owner work weren't appealing.

"Thought I heard a boat at the bank." Jonas limped toward her from the higher elevation of his house. "To what do we owe this pleasure?"

She held up the plastic containers. "I brought you something."

"Those wouldn't be pies, would they?"

She grinned. "I made them from Aunt Sophies recipe."

"Well, come on up to the house. I'll put on a pot of coffee. Or tea if you'd rather."

"Coffee sounds good."

They trudged up the bank to the yard, where a weathered picnic table sat under an ancient tree and half a dozen blossoming staked tomato plants grew toward the sun. Tall conifers grew in a row along the north side of the lot, while at least thirty peony bushes, heavily laden with buds in the first stages of opening, grew in front of them.

"Oh, they're beautiful!" she exclaimed and went to look more closely. She knelt with the pie containers balanced on her knees to lean in and smell the buds. "They're my favorite flower."

Jonas stood beside her and reached to take the containers. "They were Rebecca's too. She planted all of those. Red up by the house, then pinks and white farthest away. She was quite a gardener."

"I remember her." Kendra straightened and she followed him toward the house, hanging her hat at the top of the stair rail. "She and Aunt Sophie used to have tea in the morning."

Inside, he uncovered a pie and set it on the table with two plates and forks, then started a pot of coffee in a metal percolator on the old white enameled gas stovetop.

The kitchen was charmingly old-fashioned, which was probably chic in this day and age. She thought of the young people who would love to get their hands on the row of crocheted potholders on a wooden rack or the shelf of McCoy pottery above the pantry door. The counters held practical items like a Coleman lantern, a box of matches, and coffee cans. Hats and jackets hung on pegs by the back door. It was plain that only a man had lived here in recent years, but Rebecca Finch's touches reverently remained.

"Do you have any children?" she asked.

"No. We would have loved children but weren't meant to be."

He handed her a knife and she sliced the pie, placing generous pieces on each plate.

"Piper told us about you bein' a dancer. She said you're pretty famous."

Kendra laughed. "I'm not famous. I've been fortunate to be in a few excellent companies, and that's about it."

"But you like to teach."

"I do. Performing is exhausting. Not that I don't love it," she added quickly. "But it's involves a lot of travel. I never feel as comfortable on tour as I do at the lake."

He nodded. "The lake gets in yer blood, don't it?" He poured their coffee. "Sugar or milk? Don't have none of that other fancy stuff."

"This is perfect. I don't need fancy stuff."

Jonas sat and tasted the rhubarb pie. He sighed and nodded. "As good as I remember Sophie's."

"That's a huge compliment."

"That ring you got from Liz Cavanaugh's boy. That was pretty fancy."

She swallowed. Of course, he'd bring up the ring he'd found and returned. How he'd found it—that he'd found it at all was a curious story. "It's a beautiful ring."

"Meant a lot to you."

"It did once, yes."

"What happened?"

She thought over how she could be honest and not sound unkind. "Dusty did something I couldn't see past, something so big and hurtful, I still can't see past it."

"Does that somethin' have anythin' to do with that little tow-headed boy Liz brings with her on occasion?"

He was perceptive. And rumors had probably circulated for years. Kendra sipped her coffee. It was strong and delicious. Better than any barista coffee she'd tasted. "It did."

He nodded and drank half his brew, even though it was

still nearly scalding. He set down the mug. "How did you meet him?"

"Dusty?" She tapped a nail against her mug, thinking. "We went to school together, of course, sometimes in the same class, sometimes not. But the school was smaller back then, and the kids all pretty much knew each other. Joe was older, but I knew him, and Crosby was younger, but I remember him as well. In about fifth grade, Dusty asked me to come over to their place for a picnic." She ate a few bites of her pie. "My mom was gone a lot. Working, doing whatever else she wanted. My sister was off doing her own thing, too. The Cavanaughs sort of took me in, and after that I was welcome at their home all the time."

"They're good people."

She nodded. "I'd never been around a family before. Not one like that. They did chores, said grace before dinner, played games, watched TV together. They had grandparents and cousins and pets, and throughout junior high it was easy to pretend I was one of them. That I belonged. In high school things changed between Dusty and me. He dated a couple of girls, and I knew I didn't like that. I went to a dance or two with another boy, and he told me he didn't like that. After that, we only saw each other, and by my junior year, it was serious."

"You loved 'im?"

She looked at Jonas and nodded. It felt strange to talk to someone about this. She'd had the pain bottled inside for so long, but it felt good to say the words, and Jonas lent a sympathetic ear. "I loved him. He asked me to marry him after we'd finished college, and of course I said yes. We planned what kind of wedding we'd have. He wanted to design our home and be the contractor. We both wanted children. We had our whole future planned out."

She laid down her fork. "We were so young. And I was

foolish enough to think that fairy tale would come true. It
didn't." She changed the subject. "How did you meet
Rebecca?"

He pushed his empty plate away. "We went to school
together too. She was twelve the first time I took notice of
her. Me, being a mature worldly thirteen-year-old, well, I
chased her home with a grasshopper." Jonas paused in his
memory to erupt with a laugh. His cheeks wrinkled all the
more. "Her mother heard her squealin' and sprang from the
house with a cuttin' board. She chased me off right quick
that day."

Kendra joined his laughter.

"Rebecca and me, we laughed about that day all the years
after, picturin' Julia Wilder in her housedress and apron, a
red kerchief on her head, chasing me clean down Silverville
Road. Weren't paved back then, just a dirt road. Miz Wilder,
she used to laugh with us, though, 'cause she was the first one
to tell Rebecca, 'He's sweet on you. He wouldn't be chasing
you if he wasn't.'"

"And you were."

"Oh, yes, I was. Don't a day go by I don't wish she was
here or I was with her."

His words brought tears to Kendra's eyes. It was hard to
lose people, no matter the situation.

"How would you change your situation if you could?" he
asked, surprising her.

She sat in silence, staring at the faded red gingham
curtains. Nearby a gull's high-pitched cry broke the silence.
She couldn't change things, but if she had the power, how
would she? "I'd go back to before, I guess."

"Would that help? Would you see it coming?"

"I don't know." She picked up the plates and carried them
to the stained enamel sink. "Maybe instead, I'd just make
myself able to forgive."

"And forget?"

"Maybe." She turned back to him. "I've never talked about this to anyone."

"Prob'ly you needed to."

"Probably I did." She experienced the tug of a personal connection, an affinity of sorts, and the bond surprised her. Kendra felt entirely safe sharing things with this white-haired old man. His bone-deep kindness was apparent in everything he said, in the way he listened without judgment, and the way he seemed to understand. "I'd better get back. I have a class this afternoon."

"You come on over any time you like. I'm mostly always here iffin' I'm not at the VFW or sometimes the Frid'y night barbeque. Thank you much for the pies. I'd better freeze the extra so's I don't eat it all tonight."

"When you run out, let me know," she answered. "My freezer is getting full of rhubarb."

"I'll do that."

Outside, she plopped her hat on her head, and he walked with her across the yard and down the bank.

"Who owns the place north of Joe Cavanaugh?" she asked.

"It's had been a rental since Ben Rumford has been at Pine Valley. Ever' day I thank my lucky stars I'm right here. I might be alone, but I still have all my faculties and I ain't stuck at that senior center. I can still troll the lake, catch fish and visit my buddies."

"Not to mention return rings."

He chuckled. "That too." He waved her off as she started the engine and headed back home.

❧

Kendra found parking by the veterinarian's office. The sign reading 'Jackson Samuels, DVM' listed office hours, indicating the vet's had been closed since five. She walked across Brook Park Road to the lush green park that covered two city blocks at the center of Spencer's main business district. It hadn't been difficult to locate where the festivities were happening. Laughter and music came from an area west of the enormous white gazebo, the structure under which she remembered high school bands playing during holiday celebrations. The mouth-watering aroma of grilled meat and barbecue sauce wafted on the warm summer air.

She'd worn a coral and teal patterned cotton dress and comfortable sandals, and she carried a stack of rhubarb pies. The dollar store had provided her a resource for convenient containers that she didn't mind leaving behind.

After a class earlier in the week, Kendra had checked her phone and found a message from Piper Newport. They had exchanged numbers the night they met at the VFW.

Hey! Friday night let's hang at Brook Park.
    Volunteer firefighters cook up a mean BBQ
    6:30 See you there?

Kendra had tried to think of a reason to say she couldn't make it. But Piper was the sweetest person ever, and Kendra hadn't wanted to be rude. Finally, she'd typed a quick reply to say she'd be there. Now she neared the noisy gathering and wondered what she'd been thinking.

The first person to spot her was Cora Becker, known as Aunt Cora to the locals. She owned a cluttered antique shop and had been president of the Spencer Historical Society since its development.

"Kendra!" she called and waved with a smile. She was willowy, taller than Kendra, and wore a patterned flowing skirt, brightly-embroidered silk top and Birkenstocks, with vintage turquoise jewelry at her neck and wrists. She had been boho-chic before boho-chic was a thing. "I'd heard you were here for the summer. Let me help you with those."

"Thank you."

"You're more than welcome, dear." Her gray hair was gathered on the back of her head, revealing dangling earrings that matched her necklace. "And you're teaching again, I understand."

"I am."

"The food tables are over here. Would these by any chance be pies like your Aunt Sophie made?"

Kendra grinned. Apparently, Aunt Sophie's pies were legendary. "They are."

"I don't mind telling you I've lived seventy-two years and have never tasted a better pie. I can't wait to try a slice." They set the containers among various plates, bowls and covered dishes. She glanced around. "Zoe! Look who's here."

Zoe Barlow turned from a small gathering and joined them.

"Zoe, do you remember Kendra Price?"

Zoe was a Spencer, one of Jakob's daughters. She had a younger sister, Miranda, Kendra vaguely remembered. It almost surprised Kendra to see Zoe at a gathering like this, but she remembered the sisters as friendly and not at all stuck up, unlike some of the other Spencers.

"I remember, yes," Zoe said and took her hand. "I remember Sophie bringing you to events. You were the cutest little thing, with that gorgeous curly hair. You've grown into quite a beauty."

Kendra felt her cheeks warm. "Thank you."

"Kendra dances," Aunt Cora said to Zoe. "She has performed with some very prestigious troupes."

"Of course!" Zoe said. "There was a piece about you in the *Herald*."

"There was?" Kendra asked in surprise.

"Oh, yes. Local girl on the big stage and all that. Actual news. Cale Hartwood probably thought it would impress the tourists." She tilted her head. "It probably did. I'm impressed." She grinned.

"Zoe has a bed and breakfast to the west on Valley View Road," Cora told her. "Keeps her hoppin' from what I hear."

"Does it ever," Zoe replied. "Seems like I barely have one meal cleared away and it's time to prepare another. I'm looking for help."

"She has a handsome son, as well. Ryder is a horse wrangler for movies."

"He lives in California," Zoe added. "I expect him home for a visit this fall."

Liz and Stephanie Cavanaugh approached, carrying bags of chips and a watermelon. Steph set down the melon and gave Kendra a hug. "I'm so glad you're here. This has become a Friday night tradition."

"Good food and handsome firemen are a heady combination," Aunt Cora teased. "And there's beer."

"Piper invited me, but I haven't seen her yet."

"Well, I've been looking for you," Piper said, joining them with her grandfather in tow.

Kendra greeted Jonas's friend. "Hello, Mr. Newport."

"Everyone calls me Harm," he said.

Liz gestured toward the bandstand. "When it's time to eat, why don't you join us? We have blankets laid out over there."

Piper glanced at Kendra and then back at Liz. "Okay, sounds great."

Aunt Cora and Zoe had moved on to greet someone else.

"If it's all the same to you girls, I'll go find my pals," Harm said. "Jeeter brings chairs."

"Sure, Grandpa. Enjoy yourself."

Kendra glanced around. Where there were one or two Cavanaughs, there were sure to be more. Last time they'd parted, she'd put off having a conversation with Dusty, and she still didn't want to talk to him. She didn't want him asking again either. What good would it do to talk? The past was the past, and no amount of yapping could change it.

Piper led her to the line of smokers and grills, where half a dozen extremely fit men in royal blue SFD volunteer T-shirts slathered sauce on slabs of ribs. There were also steaks, brats and burgers. The men turned choicely cooked meat out onto enormous rectangle trays, where hungry townsfolk waited to fill their plates.

She and Piper split a steak and a brat, then filled their plates with salads and found the Cavanaughs. Ian sat beside his cousin Kyle, and when he spotted her, motioned her over. She and Piper greeted Chloe and Avery and settled in to eat.

"My dad's bringin' drinks," Ian told her.

Sure enough, dressed in faded and worn jeans, a snug-fitting Timberline Outfitters T-shirt and a straw cowboy hat, Dusty rolled two large coolers toward the gathering, unstacked them, and opened the lids. "Call it out!"

"Root beer!" Ian shouted, above his cousins.

"Orange!"

"Cola!"

Dusty delivered beverages to the kids first and then the adults. With raised brows, he held bottles of beer toward Kendra and Piper. They nodded and he placed sweating cold bottles in their hands. After closing the lids on the coolers, he settled himself in an available spot between his mom and Jackson Samuels, who Kendra hadn't noticed sitting there until now.

Jack gave her a friendly wink.

"I saw the sign. He's a veterinarian now?" she asked Piper in a quiet tone.

"Yes. Nice guy. Single." She grinned at Kendra. "His office is behind us on Brook Park Road."

She nodded. "I parked in front of it."

"His grandmother is Willa Samuels. She has that studio on the other side of the park across from us."

"Oh, the painter."

"Yes. She raised him after his parents died."

"If I ever knew that, I'd forgotten."

Kendra had run into people in Pearl's café, the bookstore, the grocery store, and some of them she remembered from her childhood, but not many. But she'd never done this—socialized. Never subjected herself to being seen and recognized. Her family association was humiliating. Just as she knew facts about people in Spencer, a lot of them knew her family. Probably her story. She glanced at Dusty again. Not from him, however. The Dusty she'd known wouldn't have broken confidentiality.

She and Piper enjoyed their meal and talked. Liz joined them and visited. Others got up and mingled in the crowd, and eventually she and Piper separated. Kendra walked around the park admiring the well-tended beds of flowers, occasionally stopping to speak with someone. She found Chloe with two of the other girls from her dance class and talked to them for quite a while. They peppered her with questions about the troupes she'd performed with and the performances. Their eager hopefulness was an inspiration and a joy.

As the sun lowered behind the mountains, a band set up on the platform in the gazebo and warmed up. A wide concrete path circled the exterior of the white structure, and she returned to stand on the path, listening to the instruments and eventually recognizing a song. The players were surprisingly good with a definite country leaning. One of the firemen who'd been at the grills sang, *Look What God Gave Her.*

Strings of white lights crisscrossing the celling of the gazebo came on. A few couples climbed the stairs and danced inside the perimeter under the shelter. Others gathered on the walkway around the outside. Kendra stepped back onto the grass and stood farther away, enjoying the songs. She loved all kinds of music. This band of three young men, an older one, and a woman, played with smiles on their faces, obviously enjoying themselves. Their music probably provided them the same joy she got from dancing.

The song changed, the rhythm slowed, and the man's deep voice sang, *"It's amazing how you can speak right to my heart. Without saying a word, you can light up the dark."*

Kendra shivered and hugged herself. As darkness fell, the air had grown cooler.

"Cold?" Dusty's voice beside her surprised her.

She glanced up at him, still wearing his hat, his face visible in the lights. "Not really. It feels nice."

"Ian hasn't let up about using your boat. Will this Saturday work for you? If the offer is still on, of course."

"Yes, of course. This week is fine. Whenever you want to use it."

"Thanks." He reached for her hand. "How about a dance?"

Her heart skittered crazily, and she chastised herself. "Oh, I don't know—"

"Do you remember how I used to be intimidated to dance with you?"

His hand was large and warm around hers. She liked the feeling too much. "I remember."

"I was legit petrified. I knew you liked me, and we were a couple, but you were a professional dancer—amazing really —and I have two left feet."

"You don't have two left feet."

"I felt like it when I was with you."

"But you got over that."

"I did. You were always so genuine. So tolerant, I guess. Receptive. One day I just realized you didn't care if I was a good dancer or not. You just wanted to be with me."

His revelation elicited a pang of emotion. She nodded. She had wanted to be with him. That's all she'd ever wanted. Her throat tightened with the memories, with the feelings.

He tugged, only a little, but she went along with him to the pavement, and he wrapped his arm around her back and held her left hand up against his chest as they fell into an easy step.

This moment might have been six or eight years ago, for the well-being she felt in his arms. She wished it was. She wished she could erase everything that had happened between then and now. They would dance with her head resting under his chin until it got late. And then they would find a spot on the north bank of Twin Owl Lake, leave the radio on and steam up the windows of his car. She'd kiss him like there was no tomorrow and they'd plan the rest of their lives together. Back then it had all been so simple. She'd been filled with hope and promise.

Dusty brought the hand on her back up to her hair and tangled his fingers in the length. She didn't change her position, in fact, she might have inched a little closer against him.

"You smell so good," he said against her ear.

A shiver tingled along her nerve-endings. He smelled like sunshine and freshly-washed cotton, with a faint woodsy scent. He held her hand pressed between their bodies and she could feel the steady beat of his heart. She closed her eyes and did something she never let herself do—she let herself feel.

Dusty loved this woman with all his heart and soul. He

would do anything to have her love him again. Beneath his fingers, her hair was thick and satin soft. She smelled as good as he remembered, felt even better in his arms. He'd dreamed of this...prayed for it.

He couldn't resist bringing up his fingers and threading them against her scalp. He raised her hand up to his lips and pressed a kiss to her slender fingers. She slid her hand from his and rested her palm as lightly as a feather along his cheek.

He felt her touch throughout his entire body. "Kendra," he whispered, his voice thick with emotion.

When he lowered his lips to hers, she didn't move away. Instead, she leaned into him and met the kiss...warm... delightfully sweet....

He'd done nothing to deserve this. Just the opposite, in fact. She was a gift, her kiss precious. Undeserved. That's how he'd always thought of her—as someone precious he didn't deserve. He ached to tell her he loved her. Saying the words right now would be the most honest, most natural thing in the world. But she didn't want to hear them. She didn't believe them. They were only words.

Actions spoke louder.

She inched back and studied his face, dropped her hand to his chest. And then, self-consciously, she took a full step away, glanced to the side at the other couples. He looked, too. No one had taken any notice of them. It took all of his gentlemanly reserve to release her. "Thank you for the dance."

"Dusty."

He waited for her next words.

"I'd better go."

He'd hoped she had something more to say to him. "Think about coming fishing with us. Ian would enjoy it."

"I don't know."

"Just think about it."

She turned and walked away from the gazebo, away from the circle of light, until he could no longer see her among the clusters of townspeople still visiting under the moon and by the light of dozens of lanterns…people eating rhubarb pie.

He was going to go see if there was any left.

CHAPTER 7

a million books were available for order online, but there was something wonderfully fulfilling about entering a well-stocked store and browsing, touching, reading covers. Kate Michaels had called out a greeting as soon as Kendra had opened the front door and the shop bell rang.

She waved to the pretty young shop owner and found a display of summer reading selections, among them a couple of her favorite authors. She read book jackets inside and out and selected a couple.

Kate joined her. "Can I help you find anything?"

"I'm just browsing for my summer reading."

"You sure look familiar. You're not a tourist, are you?"

"No, I have a house on the east end of the lake. I'm here every summer." She shifted the books to one arm and extended a hand. "Kendra Price."

"Of course, the dancer."

Gossip traveled fast in a small community. She nodded.

"Here, I'll start a pile for you by the register." She took the books.

"Thanks. Can you personally recommend anything?"

"What's your preference? Thriller? Women's fiction? Biography?"

"A little of each, I'm thinking."

Kate carried away the books and returned to show her a few recommendations. Kendra chose three to add to her pile. "That should get me through a few weeks."

"Good choices. I'll ring them up for you. Would you like a cup of coffee? I just brewed a fresh pot. No charge."

"I smelled it when I came in. That sounds nice. Thanks."

"Creamers and toppings are on the counter over there by the seating area."

Kendra paid, thanked her for the coffee and took a seat to enjoy the brew and browse through her new books.

She became absorbed in a story about three women living on the same street, all with a dark secret. She loved how fiction carried her away from her own life to live someone else's for a few hours. Whether worse or better lives than hers, stories always opened her eyes to the plights of others and gave her fresh perspectives. She turned a page and caught movement from the corner of her eye.

A mature woman wearing paint-smeared white capris with matching spattered Keds and a kerchief over her hair stood beside her chair, holding a takeout cup of coffee. "Sorry to interrupt your reading, dear."

Kendra closed her book with her thumb holding her place. "It's okay."

"I asked Kate if that was you sitting over here, and she affirmed it was."

"Have we met?"

"A long time ago. Your Aunt Sophie was a dear friend of mine."

Seems her aunt had a friend list of hundreds in this town.

She smiled a greeting. "I'm Willa Samuels. I have a studio

two blocks over." She perched on the nearest chair. She had lovely short silver hair and sparkling violet eyes. Kendra liked her immediately. "My grandson is—"

"The veterinarian."

Willa smiled. "You've met him?"

"I remembered him from the band in high school, then recently I saw him at the VFW, and he was at the barbecue the other night. I don't think I ever knew he was your grandson though. I'm still piecing together all the relationships."

"So am I. And some of them are still surprising me." She sipped her coffee. "Was Sophie quite a bit older than your mother?"

No one had mentioned her mother to her since she'd been here. "Yes. They were actually stepsisters, but I was very close to Sophie. She was more like a…." She shouldn't say mother, but she hadn't been like a grandmother. "She was down-to-earth and practical. Kind. She taught me to love dance. I wouldn't be who I am today if not for her."

Saying those words to a stranger embarrassed her, and the turbulent feelings brought to the surface were even more embarrassing.

"We all need someone like that." Willa leaned over to pat her knee. "You've traveled. Have you been to Paris?"

"Once."

"I studied art there when I was young. The experience of a lifetime, but I could never leave this place. We have everything a person might want, from the solitude of the lakes and mountains to casual barbeques and fancy social events at the lodge. We're a shout away from the national park, and majestic beauty is everywhere. This place is an artist's dream."

"I'm with you on the solitude part."

Willa gave her a wink. "Watch it. These people will grow on you."

They already were, and Kendra didn't know how she felt about that. "You're probably right."

"I know I am." She stood. "It's a pleasure to see you. Come by my studio soon."

"I will."

Willa and Kate spoke, and the bell over the shop door rang as the woman left. Strange that the only people she didn't like in this town were her own family. But she had no cause to see them, so as long as she stayed her course, things might go smoothly.

She still needed to shop for groceries. Her baking supplies had been depleted, so she gathered her things, thanked Kate, and set out to finish running her errands. Heading east on Second Street, she spotted several enormous elk crossing Brook Park Road, heading her way and away from the park. She stopped her car and waited as they rambled past in the direction she'd come. Behind her to the south were campgrounds and the Gold River. It wasn't unusual to see these animals with their impressive antlers on the streets and in the parks. Since it was summer, they didn't have dark neck manes, so their bodies were all tan-colored. The males likely weighed seven hundred pounds, making them appear intimidating this close. She glanced around, noting no one was on the sidewalks. People pretty much left the elk alone when they wandered into Spencer.

She wondered what Ian thought of seeing wild animals like this as part of his normal life. Children born in Spencer grew up with a respect for the living creatures whose wilderness had been invaded by civilization. Parents and teachers taught their kids safety as well as regard for the animals. Strange how now that he had a name and a face and a personality, thoughts of the boy came to mind often. For so long his existence had been the object of her disappointment and heartbreak. She felt bad for that now.

Since Dusty had mentioned bringing his son out to her place on Saturday, she'd thought of little else. Any time spent around Dusty only reminded her of what she'd lost, and she wasn't prone to torturing herself. Dancing with him—that sweet kiss—had been the source of her difficulty sleeping every night since. She didn't want to stay angry. She detested those feelings, but the alternative? Losing her protective anger might be worse in the long run. As long as she resented him, blamed him, nursed the hurt, she protected herself. Letting down her guard, now that would be dangerous.

❦

On Saturday she woke before first light, selected music, flipped on the strands of lights strung across the ceiling of her studio and warmed up. The reflections in the darkness, were so pretty, she made a video to send to her manager later. The woman could do amazing things with bits of film for promotion and marketing.

She showered, made two pans of zucchini-rhubarb bread, and was dressed in her old jeans and a cropped T-shirt when the ratchety *br-r-ring* of the old-fashioned front bell sounded.

"It's not locked! Come on in." She set the pans on racks to cool and pulled off her oven mitts.

"Why wasn't your door locked?" Dusty asked, entering the kitchen, with Ian at his side.

"Because I knew you were coming early."

"It sure smells good in here." Ian stood on tiptoe to look in the pans.

"Those are hot, but I'll send a loaf home with you later," she told him.

"Can I see the rest of your house?"

"Ian—"

"It's fine," she told Dusty. "How about I show you around while your dad gets the fishing gear loaded?"

Dusty headed outside, and she showed Ian the other rooms.

"What's up there?" he asked, peering up the narrow staircase.

He smelled like coconut oil sunscreen. "My studio. Head on up."

She followed him up the stairs. He stood in the large open room and looked around. "It sure is big, but there's not much in here."

"Plenty of room to dance is all."

"Can I see you dance?"

She led him over to the tripod and removed the camera, rewinding the recording and playing it for him on the four-inch screen. "I shot it this morning. I use this camera for remembering choreography and for publicity videos."

Ian watched the clip with interest. "What's choralography?"

"Choreography is a dance routine, sequences of steps and movements all put together and memorized."

"It sounds hard."

"It is hard, but so is anything worth doing right."

"Learning to write my name was real hard," he told her, with a serious expression. "I had the longest name of all the whole class."

"I'll bet you did. Can you write it now?"

"Yep. I remeberized it."

"Good job. That's how I remember dance steps too."

"You two comin'?" Dusty called from below.

Ian looked at her, his blue eyes wide and serious. "We dug up worms. They're in a pail."

"Well, let's go get them."

He clambered down the stairs with her following, to run past his dad toward the door. "Did you get the worms?"

"I did. Let's go out the side door."

"You coming?" Dusty asked her.

She reached for her straw hat and her bag. "You got enough worms?"

"Do you remember how to tie knots?" he countered.

They'd always had a running competition on the correct knot to use. He fastened an orange life vest on Ian, pulled out caps for both of them, and the three climbed into the boat he'd already lowered onto the water. Dusty sat at the rear and steered the boat onto the lake.

"There's Uncle Joe's place."

Ian's gaze followed where he pointed. "Is that Chloe? Chloe!" His voice carried across the water.

The small figure in the distance, waved to them. She was on the back dock, probably reading or napping in the sun.

Dusty headed the runabout to the west, where there were inlets, carefully skirting shallow areas. He turned off the engine. They baited and cast their lines, then waited. The echo of the motor had disappeared, replaced by the sounds of birds and insects.

"Did Grandpa Sam take you fishin', Daddy?" Ian asked.

"He took all of us kids fishing," he answered. "One or two at a time. Even though there were a lot of us, he had a way of making each one of us feel special."

"Did he teach you to tie knots?"

"Yep."

"Did your dad take you fishin'?" The boy directed his question to Kendra.

She didn't even pause in her reply. "My Aunt Sophie took me fishing and taught me to tie knots."

"Wow."

"She taught me to bake. And how to dance."

His gaze went from his pole to her. "Not your mom?"

"No."

"What did your mom teach you?"

Kendra didn't look at Dusty. "How to be independent."

"What's that mean?"

"Take care of myself."

"My mom wanted my dad to take care of me and teach me stuff, din't she, Dad?"

"Yes," Dusty answered. She couldn't see his eyes under the bill of his cap.

How was it she'd never wondered before what Dusty had told Ian about his situation—about his mother? He had a mother who hadn't wanted any part of him or his life. She knew how the lack of a mother's love could mess up someone. Of course, he had a caring, loving father, wonderful grandparents and extended family—he was obviously deeply loved. But one day he'd realize his mother just plain hadn't wanted the bother of a child—of him.

Her chest ached with the thought.

She'd never realized how self-centered nursing her own pain had been.

But she didn't give Erica much thought. Ignoring her existence was better for Kendra's peace of mind. But looking at this little boy, so full of life and energy and love, she couldn't help thinking of the truly selfish person who had given birth to him.

Would she be happier if Erica was in his life? No. So why did she care?

She cared for his sake. She cared for the young man he would become. She didn't want to—and she resented the feelings—but all the same she cared.

Something tugged at her line, and she focused her attention on reeling it in. "I've got a bite!"

"You got a fish!" Ian called and pointed for his dad to look.

"What is it?" Dusty asked as she brought it up out of the water.

She got it inside the boat. "Looks like a yellow perch, doesn't it?"

Dusty moved the bucket toward her, and she dislodged the hook and placed her catch in the pail of water.

"I'm getting the next one," he said firmly.

"Or me," Ian disagreed.

"Or you."

During the next few hours Ian caught two small brown trout and Dusty got a large rainbow. Kendra and Dusty each reeled in a good-sized brown. But Kendra learned a lot about Ian. The child chattered almost non-stop, talking about his friends from preschool and daycare, his Sunday school teacher, their neighbor's cat, Mr. Big, the fact that he hated olives, his new socks that he didn't like, and all about his favorite cartoons. And the questions never ended.

"Do you think Adam named that a rainbow trout 'cause it's has those shiny scales all diff'ernt of colors? Mrs. Cantu said God told Adam to name all the animals on his very own. That must have been a big job. Do you think all those animals were loose in the garden, like the tigers and lions too? There musta been elks walking all over too, like here. It musta been crowded."

She glanced at Dusty to find him checking her reactions from beneath the bill of his cap. "I think they were," he said. "But the garden wasn't like Grandma's garden or even the Wilkins' farm. It was more like a national park. Remember I showed you how big Rocky Mountain National Park is on the map?"

Ian nodded.

She let it sink in that Dusty took his son to Sunday

school, like his parents had taken him. She'd gone a few times with neighbor kids, with the Cavanaughs.

"That must've been awesome." Ian peered back into the bucket. "Are we gonna eat 'em tonight?"

"Why don't we eat the big one and freeze the others for the fish fry at the VFW?" Dusty suggested.

"Yes, an' I can tell Jonas and Jeeter I caught 'em!"

"Boy, they will be impressed," his dad agreed with a grin.

"Can we cook 'em at your place, Kendra?" the boy asked.

"We sure can. I have a brick fireplace in the back and a big black skillet that fries up some good fish."

"Like camping!"

"Exactly like camping."

"I'll make a salad and some beans while you men clean the fish, how's that?"

It was only late afternoon as they sat on lawn chairs in the shade and ate delicious crispy fried trout, picking all the meat from the bones and licking their fingers. Kendra had a basin of sudsy water to wash their hands, and they piled the dishes on a tray.

She'd spread a blanket and Ian laid down, rubbing his eyes.

"He still takes a nap in the afternoon," Dusty said.

"He probably talks himself into exhaustion," she whispered.

"Kendra showed me a video," Ian said. "She's a good dancer."

"Yes, I know."

"How many weeks until my birthday, Daddy?"

"Only three."

"Did you get me a present yet?"

"What? Do you think you need a present for every birth-day?" His eyes twinkled as he glanced at Ian lying on the blanket.

Ian grinned at him, but his eyes drifted shut.

"I don't have beer, but how about wine?" Kendra asked after the child had dozed off.

"Sounds all right."

Heading into the house, she returned with a cold bottle and stemmed glasses. She'd already pulled the cork, so she poured them each a glass.

She gazed out over the lake. "This is my favorite place to be in the evening."

"Sorry about all the questions."

"Don't be. He's a smart little guy. He's inquisitive."

"He likes you."

"I like him." She sipped her wine. "I haven't been around children his age since Kyle and Avery were small. Do they all talk as much as he does?"

"All of them I know. My mother, the saint, hosts his birthday parties for classmates."

"Your mom is great."

Dusty had removed his shoes and slouched in the chair with his bare feet in the grass. "That she is."

"I used to love being at your house when we were young. I was overwhelmed at first, by you and your rambunctious brothers, by your parents' attention. I didn't know how to react."

"I remember." He took off his cap and ruffled his fair hair with his fingers until it stood up in shiny waves. He dropped his cap on the blanket and cradled his glass.

"And the food," she said. "Funny how I remember the food so well. I thought your family was rich." She absently drew a line down the denim over her thigh with her thumb-nail. "Fruit with every meal, and vegetables, dishes I'd never tasted. I still remember your mom's pot roast as a feast."

"You were a scrawny little thing. Mom was probably hoping to fatten you up." He leaned to pick up a twig from the grass and snapped it. "Speaking of fattening you up, she reminded me to ask you for dinner tomorrow."

Kendra filled her glass and passed the bottle to Dusty. "I'll think about it."

He poured wine into his glass. "You're thinking about a lot."

"I suppose I am."

He put the cork in the bottle and set in in the grass. "We're talking right now. It's going well. We could just as well talk about what we're avoiding."

Dusty could tell the instant he'd overstepped her comfort barrier and her demeanor changed. She sat up a little straighter in the chair, and he did too. "I'm sorry. Forget I said that."

"I haven't forgotten anything, Dusty. It's just that I need some time. Things are changing pretty quickly."

She had to keep her defenses in place, that was obvious. "I get it," he said. "You don't owe me anything."

"Yet you seem determined to extract something from me, and I'm not sure what. That's what scares me."

He shook his head. "I don't want anything from you."

"You want my forgiveness—my approval. You want to absolve yourself."

He stretched an arm toward her chair. "I don't. You're wrong. I don't expect anything like that. You can't give what you don't have."

She didn't know what to say to that. To any of it. "I'm going to take in these dishes and wrap up the loaves of bread, so Ian can take one home."

He nodded and watched her load a tray and carry it to the house.

What did he want from her? He'd lived with this for nearly six years, and he didn't know what he wanted. Until she'd come back this time, his situation had begun to feel normal. There were other single fathers—Matt Chandler, the outfitter for the lodge was a single dad, though he was a widow, and that was certainly different. Other children had been given into the custody of their fathers. But he wanted a wife, he wanted Ian to have a mother. The missing element was never as evident as when his family was together, but that was also where Ian got all the love and acceptance that made him a confident well-adjusted child. Dusty loved Ian more than his own life. He'd do anything for him, anything to protect him. Would that have to mean putting Kendra behind him?

He'd never stopped loving her, not for a moment, but he couldn't see a way for this situation to change. What was done was done. Maybe there was nothing more to say. What were words to her?

His son rolled over and sleepily blinked up at him. "Hey, Daddy."

"Hey, my little man. You about ready to pack up and go home?"

❦

Joe had offered, but Kendra drove herself to Liz's the following afternoon. Steph had spent the previous afternoon preparing lasagnas that only needed to be baked before dinner. After an early trip to the farmer's market that morning, Kendra had changed up her game and made pies—apple, strawberry and peach. All that was required was to make salads and set the table.

The others had apparently met Crosby's dinner companion previously, a brunette with short-cropped hair and a jeweled stud in her nose. Brianna seemed to have more in common with Chloe and Avery than the other women, because the three of them played games on their phones after prep was finished.

"I figured out you all know Brianna already," Kendra said quietly to Steph.

"They've been on and off for over a year," the dark-haired young woman replied. "The workings of his mind are a little scary. Sometimes I think he just invites someone to Sunday dinner, so he can't be pressured into a serious conversation."

They had finished the meal and pie had been served to everyone's appreciation when Grandma Naomi asked Dusty to go into the other room and get a bag she'd brought with her. "The big one with flowers," she clarified. "And Tyler, come help me to that comfortable chair in the other room. I want all of you to join me. The dishes can wait."

The family obeyed her instructions and gathered around her as though she held court, some on nearby chairs, others seated on the floor.

"I asked your mother and my niece Zoe, to help me with a project that had been hanging over my head," she said, her voice strong. "After your grandfather died, your parents and my other son packed much of our belongings and put them in storage so I could move into a smaller home. I didn't want all that to be left to others when I'm gone, so my niece has been bringing me boxes and I've slowly been going through things."

"We would have helped you, Grandma," Joe told her.

She waved a bony hand. "I know you would have, but I wanted to see it all myself and make decisions. And maybe surprise some of you." She leaned forward. "Help me with these, Dustin."

Dusty opened the enormous satchel for her inspection.

She pointed. "That one." Taking a slim square black case, she opened it and held it toward Liz. "These are for you."

Liz drew close to accept it and lifted a pearl necklace

from the case, her expression indeed showing surprise. "I don't know what to say, Naomi. I remember you wore this necklace to our wedding." She rolled the pearls between her fingers. "You've worn these for many years."

"And you will wear them for many years too," the elderly woman said with a nod.

"Thank you." Liz bent to press her cheek against her mother-in-law's and then resumed her seat.

One by one, Naomi went through the contents of the satchel, giving her grandchildren special mementos and her blessing. Dusty received a pocket watch that had been his great-grandfather's. Ian came into possession of a box of rare baseball cards. The girls received brooches and earrings, and Chloe unfolded a beautiful deep-blue satin shawl with embroidery and fringe that Naomi's cousin brought her from Korea after World War II.

Naomi had even impressively prepared ahead for Crosby's date-of-the-week, who good-naturedly accepted a rhinestone tiara. Kendra was impressed with the elderly woman's thoughtfulness and care with each gift.

"And for you, my dear," Naomi said, gesturing Kendra close and handing her a rose-patterned, paper-covered box.

Kendra knelt in front of her and accepted the gift with a smile, prepared to be amused.

"Open it," Naomi urged.

She lifted the lid away, finding the interior papered as well, and the contents hidden in tissue. Gingerly, she turned back the paper and gazed upon a pair of white satin slippers. The others were waiting silently to see what she revealed. Hesitantly, she lifted one slipper out of the box. The shoe had intricate embroidery, with a silk rose across the toe and a small heel. Kendra blinked and turned her gaze up to Naomi.

The elderly woman's faded blue eyes sparkled, and Kendra imagined they had been bright like Dusty's at one time. Naomi smiled, deepening the slashes beside her mouth and the lines around her eyes. "They were my dancing slippers for my wedding. I wore them for our first dance when my Harold and I glided across the floor with eyes for no one but each other. I only wore them that one night."

Kendra blinked back the sting of moisture in her eyes. "But they're so special. Are you sure you want me to have them?"

Close by, Liz's tiny sob was audible.

"I'm absolutely sure," Naomi told her. "*You're* special, and I don't ever want you to forget that. There's a lot of love in those old shoes, and probably a few good dances left, too."

Kendra rose on her knees to put her arms around Naomi's frail shoulders. "This gift is so thoughtful," she whispered. "I'm going to treasure them."

"You're the treasure," the old woman whispered back. And then she released her and waved at her granddaughters. "Go help your grandma with dishes now."

Her orders brought a few chuckles and lightened the mood. Their grandmother's gifts had obviously reminded each of them how frail she was and that they were enjoying their last years with her now.

Kendra carefully wrapped the wedding slippers and stowed them in the box. She'd been sincere about what a thoughtful gift Naomi had selected for her. Right up there with the engagement ring Dusty had chosen and the house Aunt Sophie had willed to her and her sister.

She couldn't meet Dusty's eyes. What did he think of his grandmother giving her wedding shoes to Kendra? Would there be a special treasure remaining for his wife one day?

She didn't want to think like that. She didn't want to consider Dusty falling in love with another woman and marrying her, bringing her into Ian's life.

But it wasn't up to her what Dusty did or didn't do. She

had no say in his life or in Ian's. She wasn't the crying type, prided herself on her ability to tough it out through difficult situations, so the fact that she felt very much like crying right now confused her and made her angry with herself.

Her unaccustomed emotional reaction to a gift from Dusty's grandmother surprised her, but she recognized why. She'd fabricated a bomb-worthy shell to prevent her from self-pity and loneliness. Self-protection had served her well all her life so far, and she wasn't going to let an old pair of wedding slippers crack that protection.

What was she doing here then?

CHAPTER 8

When Dusty brought him to use her boat for fishing, Kendra heard all about Ian's birthday party with his friends. She didn't go with them, because she had videos to watch and performance notes to make before Monday's class.

"You're coming to dinner tomorrow, aren't you?" Dusty asked once they'd returned the boat and presented her with a cleaned rainbow trout as their way of saying thanks. "It's our family party. We celebrate Ian and Brooke's birthdays together."

"Your mom mentioned it to me." She took Ian's empty glass and watched him run across her front lawn after a ground squirrel. "She also told me Ian's grandmother would be there. I'm going to take a hard pass."

"He'll wonder why you don't come."

"There will be plenty of family there. I won't be missed."

"That's not true."

"You know how I feel about her, Dusty. She's his—grandmother." The word was hard to say. "I'm nothing to him."

"That's not true. You're special to him."

"He has plenty of special people who will be there."

He handed her his glass and picked up his tackle box. "I respect your right to make your own decisions. You're welcome if you change your mind. Come on, Ian!"

"I got this close!" the boy said, stretching out his arms.

She grinned.

Ian ran toward her. "Thanks for letting us use your boat to go fishin'."

She set the glasses on the top step. "You're welcome."

He reached up for a hug and she knelt down to accommodate him. His arms went around her neck and he pressed his warm little body into her, his face in her neck. "Next time when all your work is done, you can go with us again. That time was the best day ever."

His declaration warmed her heart and endeared him to her even more. "Okay," she promised.

He released her and leaned back to look at her. "I get another cake tomorrow. Gramma's making a white one with strawberries on top. You can have a big piece."

Dusty was already putting their gear in his truck. She held Ian's gaze, thinking of how she could explain. "I might have work to do…."

"But you'll be done in time for my party, won't you?" He leaned forward and whispered loudly, "Aunt Steph is bringing a pony for us to ride, but it's a secret."

"If it's a secret, how do you know?"

He frowned a moment and then brightened. "My cousins are pretty bad at secrets."

She laughed.

"You can see me ride it!"

She reached to hold his shoulders a moment and run her hands down his sturdy little arms. How did anyone ever tell this child no? "I can't wait to see you ride the pony. And I'll keep your secret."

He grinned, showing off his row of small white teeth. She hoped he never had to experience disappointment in his life, but no one could protect a child from everything. She trusted Dusty to raise him in such a way that he would learn how to overcome obstacles and disenchantments without losing his love for life and people.

Ian ran to his father and Dusty lifted him into the back seat of the crew cab. Her heart weighed heavily in her chest. Was this how parents felt? How parents should feel? Protective. Concerned. Hopeful. She understood Dusty a little better. Understood he'd changed his life to be responsible for his child. She respected that.

Kendra excelled at putting things out of her mind. She finished preparing her videos and lessons and took the boat across the lake to visit Jonas that evening. He was glad to see her, greeted her and showed her the peonies in bloom. Before she left, he cut her a huge bouquet of the various vibrant colors and send them home with her, wrapped in wet newspaper.

After arranging them in one of Aunt Sophie's vases, she made herself comfortable on the sofa and watched *Notting Hill*, one of her favorite movies. '*I'm just a girl, standing in front of a boy....*' She fell asleep before it was over and woke early.

She'd run away so she didn't have to watch Dusty move on without her. So she didn't have to see pity in anyone's eyes or answer questions about their breakup. So she didn't have to deal with people, especially with her family. But now, because she couldn't disappoint Dusty's son, she was going to face Lacey today.

She made herself a protein shake and went upstairs to warm up and dance. A good workout always made her feel more confident. She was going to need every ounce of confidence and self-control she could muster.

❧

Brianna had accompanied Crosby again, garnering a few surprised glances.

"Hi, Kendra," she said, spotting her after Kendra had piled Ian's gift on the stack on the back patio. "I looked you up online and found a few videos. You're so talented."

"Thanks," she answered.

Brianna wore a sleeveless layered top that bared her shoulders, and she had a tattoo that ran from under the fabric at her shoulders down her left arm past her elbow to her forearm. Various flowers plus ribbons, music notes and birds, all in blues and greens with a little purple here and there. "Did you dance when you were little? My mom got me into dance, but I dropped out after a couple of years. She liked it more than I did."

"I danced from the time I was small," Kendra replied. "My aunt had a studio and taught." She'd never have danced without Sophie. Her mom hadn't cared less what she did. She glanced around, hoping her search was subtle. Lacey Price stood in the yard, talking with Liz.

Brianna noticed where her attention had gone. "Oh, that's the bartender at the Wild Card, isn't it? Lacey?"

"That's her."

"She works the new side on Friday nights. That's how I know her. I get this is a small town, but I wonder how the Cavanaughs know her."

"She's Ian's other grandmother."

"Oh." One syllable and Brianna said nothing more. Probably rolling it around in her head, trying to figure the logistics. Ian had no mother in the picture. Crosby might have told Brianna the situation, but somehow Kendra doubted that.

When her heart tripped double time, Kendra hated that

she had little control over her physical reaction. She took a few cleansing breaths to calm herself. She had as much right to be here as anyone else. The birthday boy wanted her here.

Brooke came out of the house, wearing navy-blue scrubs, and her black hair pulled into its glorious full ponytail. She even looked gorgeous in her work clothes. She spotted Kendra and Brianna. "I was supposed to be off today, but I had a flight. I barely got back in time."

"Is your patient all right?" Kendra asked.

"Yes, except for a broken leg. He was hiking to the north and took a fall. I probably still have twigs and leaves in my hair. It was quite a trek to recover him. I didn't want to miss Steph's surprise."

"You mean the rented pony?"

Brooke stared at her. "I thought it was a secret."

Kendra shrugged.

"I didn't know until now," Brianna added.

The three chuckled.

The back lawn had been set up with orderly rows of tables and chairs, and a balloon centerpiece on each table. No doubt Steph had played a part in the décor and layout of the tables and food. She was currently watching Ian and his cousins play cornhole and talking to a small girl Kendra didn't recognize.

"Who is the dark-haired little girl?" she asked.

Dusty came up beside her. "That's Madison Michaels. Her mom, Kate, owns the Rocky Mountain Bookstore. They live above the store. Kate's dad has the biggest ranch in the area. I hear he's not doing well, though."

His light blue summer shirt intensified the color of his eyes. The sight of him still took her breath away. She nodded. "I know Kate. She helped me choose my summer reading."

He gestured. "She's over there."

Dusty rested his hand on her forearm and leaned close to

her ear. "Thank you for coming. I know Ian talked you into it."

The touch on her arm and his breath on her neck created a shiver across her shoulders. She glanced up quickly and met his blue eyes. The power his nearness held over her was unmistakable. He created so many confusing emotions within her, she didn't know whether to turn and run or crush herself against him and cling for all she was worth. She hated herself for her weakness. She could keep it at bay until a situation like this arose.

His features had matured, and only for the better. His was still the face that took her breath away. His gaze moved from her eyes to her mouth, and even in this crowd, with people talking and children laughing, he stirred a yearning within her. They'd shared countless kisses, so she knew the warmth and texture of his lips on hers, how he could be achingly gentle until she pressed for more....

Heat rose up her neck and warmed her cheeks.

He took his hand from her arm.

She looked away.

Liz joined them and hugged her. "Hello, sweet girl." She took Kendra's hand. "I'm glad you came today."

"I remember what a big deal birthdays were when Kyle and Avery and Chloe were small," she said. "You even had a couple of birthday parties for me."

"April," Liz said with a nod. "It's still in my calendar."

Kendra spotted Lacey across the yard, clapping for Ian as he threw beanbags at the slanted wooden boards. Sometimes she wondered if her memory or her anger had skewed what she recalled about her childhood, but try as she might, she couldn't think of a time Lacey had bought or baked her a cake or bothered to show up for anything, let alone cheer for her. Seeing her participating in Ian's party was like stepping into an alternate universe.

"She has made every effort to be part of Ian's life," Liz told her softly. "I don't know what that must feel like to you. It has to be hard."

"I'm happy for Ian," Kendra told her without hesitation. "Every child deserves to feel special and wanted."

Liz put her arm around Kendra's shoulders. "You're right about that."

Aunt Sophie and Liz were the two people who had made her feel that way.

"I hope you see that if Lacey hadn't made this effort to know Ian and spend time with him, it wouldn't be because Ian wasn't loveable or deserving. It would be because something in her is broken and incapable."

Kendra understood. She nodded. Lacey had been broken and incapable of showing her love or attention. For the first time she let herself recognize it had been the same for Erica. Erica had deserved their mother's affection and devotion as well. She'd let anger and rejection turn her another direction, however.

Dusty's mother moved on to visit with other guests. Kendra made herself a plate of fruit and enjoyed it while she got better acquainted with Kate Michaels and a few of the others. A tall nice looking thirty-something guy with dark hair was wearing the same T-shirt she'd seen Dusty wearing —Timberline Outfitters with a horse logo. He noticed her attention and ambled toward her. "Are you the dancer?"

"Yes," she answered in surprise. "How did you know?"

"I heard someone at Pearl's mention you were in Spencer for the summer, and I remember seeing your picture in the *Herald*."

"I'm always surprised to hear that."

"I'm Matt Chandler. I was probably out of high school before you got there. Joe and I played football together."

"I probably saw a game or two then," she said. "I'm

familiar with Timberline Outfitters." A sign stood along on Forest Lake Drive, the road that led west past the neighborhood where Lacey still lived.

"Have you ever ridden?"

She shook her head. She'd heard kids talk about going on trail rides for their birthdays, but she'd never had the opportunity. "No."

"You'll have to grab a couple friends and come out sometime."

"Sure."

Sure, just grab a couple friends. That was what most people did, right?

"Those are my boys over there with Ian." He nodded toward the group of children playing games. "Zach and Stevie."

"Do they like horses too?"

"Oh yeah. They've been around the horses all their lives, so they're a big help. We always have between sixty and eighty head, so even with hired help it takes a couple of hours in the morning to feed and water them all, and longer in the evening to do the same, plus give hay. The boys help train on weekends."

This guy was easy to like right off the bat. Friendly, hardworking, proud of his children. She glanced around. "Which one is your wife?"

He cocked his head and glanced to the side before looking at her. "I'm widowed."

"Oh, I'm so sorry." She splayed her hands and then drew them back. She'd put her foot directly into her mouth. She regretted asking.

"Thanks. It's been a couple of years, but it's still not easy to say. Nikki was Jakob Spencer's granddaughter, so my kids and Ian are distant cousins—or something like that." He grinned. "I don't know, those distant relations confuse me."

Another single father. She'd become so wrapped up in her own drama and striving to move forward, it was easy to forget others had their own hurts and disappointments they had to work through every day. She wished she could express that to him, but he didn't know her, and she'd already said something awkward. "Me too. I need a family tree to figure out this family's relation to the Spencers. The relationships don't always click into place in my mind. Dusty's grandmother is Jakob's sister."

He thought a minute. "Right. Naomi Cavanaugh is Jakob Spencer's older sister." He nodded and they looked at each other. "Hey, it's okay that you asked me about my wife. It's natural."

She nodded. "I've been gone. And to be honest, I don't mix much in town, so I don't hear news."

"Not a bad thing," he replied with half a grin. "If you'll excuse me, I have a special guest to bring around."

"Sure. Great to meet you."

He disappeared around the corner of the house, and within a few minutes a shout went up from the children. Matt led a two-toned pony with a bright blue halter and small saddle toward the gathering. "Who wants a ride?"

Ian and Madison Michaels ran forward, while Zach and Stevie followed at the slower pace. They were obviously used to rides on a much larger scale, and Kendra smiled watching them help the other two get acquainted with the pony.

Ian graciously offered Madison the first ride. Her mother, Kate, wore an expression of concern, but Matt assured her the ride was perfectly safe. Still, she watched every movement and ran forward to get her daughter when the ride was over.

Ian climbed onto the pony himself. "Let go! I can ride him myself."

Dusty nodded at Matt, and Matt handed over the reins. Dusty got out his phone and took pictures.

"Dusty's a good daddy, isn't he?"

Kendra stiffened at the familiar voice from her childhood. Her head buzzed for a moment. She turned and looked at Lacey beside her.

Lacey Price had vertical smoker's lines around her bright pink-glossed lips. She wore liner and thick mascara, and there were slashes at the outer corners of her eyes. She looked older than Liz, though she was a good fifteen years younger. "I thought you might visit while you were here this summer. I guess you're too busy decorating your nice house and polishing your trophies."

"I'm teaching."

"And still coming to the Cavanaugh's."

Kendra felt a little sick. "Seems you're pretty friendly with them now too."

"I get to see Ian."

"I noticed."

"I'm his grandmother. I didn't ignore the fact that he was born."

"Lucky him."

"I'm making an effort here, Kendra. I didn't have anything to do with how this turned out, but I wanted to be a part of his life. You haven't even acknowledged he's your nephew. He's your family, and you've shut him out too."

Kendra glanced to the side, assuring they weren't over-head. Everyone was a distance away, paying attention to the kids and the pony. She looked back at Lacey. "Did you ever wonder if being part of his life would be best for him?"

"Family is important."

"Is that something you read on a needlepoint pillow five years ago and it suddenly changed your life?"

Lacey's lips tightened and she raised a hand to brush hair

behind her ear. Her wrist and fingers were bony, and guessing from the knobby knuckles, she probably suffered from a touch of arthritis. She had changed physically in the years Kendra had been gone. "I know you think I was a shitty mom. I kept a house for us. You had food and clothes. I worked and took care of that."

"No, you *were* a shitty mom. I didn't just think that up. *Sometimes* we had food, and I got all of the clothes Erica was finished with. I never had friends or birthdays or a pet, but you know, you always had half a dozen bottles of vodka stashed in your room."

"You were always so dramatic and needy. It was hard for me being alone."

Kendra couldn't let that one pass. "You did not spend all those nights alone."

"I was paying the bills and raising kids alone."

Kendra shook her head and raised both hands in a question. "Raising kids implies a lot more than what you did for us." She lowered her hands. "You playing all innocent and not accountable is why we haven't seen each other. I don't want to do this. There's no point in dredging up the past or going over what's already done. There's no changing that. There's no fixing it. You can't even compare a normal kids' life to mine and see a difference."

"I see the difference. They have money and fathers."

"Not all of them. Not every kid has money and two parents. Ian has a father, but he doesn't have a mother, because Erica wanted no part of his life—which is to his benefit, don't get me wrong—but at least he has the love and attention of one parent."

"Oh, for crying out loud. You had a great childhood. You had Sophie. You could run over there and be coddled whenever you wanted. Erica didn't have a Sophie."

This woman knew how to push all her buttons, and she

hated that she'd been sucked into the vortex. She didn't want to, but she looked Lacey in the eyes. "Yes, I did. But she wasn't my mother. *You* should have been sewing my dance costumes. *You* should have been teaching me to bake. *You* should have been going to teacher conferences. *You* should have been home in the evenings."

"I didn't have time for things that weren't earning an income. I had to work."

Kendra held up a hand and took a breath before she blew up and listed all the ways Lacey had spent her time. She dropped her hand to her side. "Your job is a life choice. There are day jobs. There are mothers who work and still have time for their kids. Erica and I played second best to the asshat of the week and your social life at the bar. No wonder we turned out the way we did." She'd just made excuses for Erica and was continuing the accusations she claimed she didn't want to make. "I am not doing this. Please. Leave me alone."

She turned with as much dignity as she could muster, walked inside and ran up the stairs to the hall bathroom and locked herself inside. She pushed her hair back with hands that trembled and looked at herself in the mirror over the sink. She didn't even know who she looked like. She resembled Lacey somewhat, but her hair and eyes were someone else's, a father she wouldn't recognize if he sat down next to her at Pearl's.

She'd let herself in for this. She was not crazy or dysfunctional, and she did not blame everyone else for her situation. She had taken control of her life, had made something of herself, had achieved dreams. Then why had she come to Spencer again? Why had she bought Aunt Sophie's house in the first place? Why did she return every summer when she could have stayed away and spared herself having to face these people?

Because somewhere deep inside, she needed to face it all.

CHAPTER 9

A tap on the door startled her. "Kendra?"

Dusty. "What?"

"I saw part of that. Are you all right?"

"What do you think?"

"Can I come in?"

She straightened, paused and moved to unlock the door. Dusty entered and closed it behind him.

She ran her fingers across her lips. "I shouldn't have come."

"You didn't want to disappoint Ian."

"He wouldn't have known if I was here or not."

"Was it bad?"

"I said things I didn't want to say."

"Maybe you needed to."

"I didn't."

"I think maybe you did."

She hugged her arms around herself. "What's wrong with me, Dusty?"

He took two steps forward and drew her against him. She unfolded her arms between them, pressed her palms against his back and her face into his chest. Her world had always stopped spinning and settled into place when he held her, and his embrace still had the same calming effect. He smelled like sunshine and maybe a little like a horse.

"I let you down," he said. "We had a plan, and a future to look forward to, but I ruined that. You could have put her behind you if not for that. You would have."

She leaned back enough to look up at him. "I've been rough on you."

"I deserved it."

"She doesn't recognize her part. She thinks she's has good reasons. She's justified because we had a house and she had a job, and she doesn't acknowledge what she did."

"Would it make a difference if she said she was sorry? If she really had regret?"

"I don't know."

"Do you want her to regret the way she was?"

"Yes." His questions were as much about himself as about her mother. She untangled herself from his arms and took a step back. She was a freaking wreck. "You need to get back to Ian,"

He released her.

She held up her hair with one hand and turned to splash cold water on her face with the other. Dusty handed her a towel. "Give me your phone."

She pulled it out of her back pocket.

He took it, then extended it for her to unlock. She did so, and he entered his phone number. "You can call or text me any time. I mean it."

She nodded. "Okay."

"You going to be okay now?"

She assured him with a nod. "I'm good."

"Are you leaving?"

"Nope. I'm going to eat cake and watch Ian open his gifts."

No one was braver or held their chin higher than Kendra Price. He was the only one in the world who knew her I-don't-give-a-crap attitude was all bluster. She was incredible. He'd never loved her more than he loved her in that moment. He allowed himself to admire her dewy skin, the shape of her lips, and that intoxicating hair for only a moment, and then he backed away and opened the door.

In the kitchen his mother was loading a tray with paper plates and plastic forks. "Is she all right?"

"She's okay."

"We did see that coming, but there was nothing we could do. Will you carry this?"

Dusty uncovered the sheet cake decorated like a lake with a miniature plastic fisherman in a boat and carried it outdoors, the tiny fish on the man's line swinging back and forth.

"It's my cake!" Ian ran forward and studied the birthday dessert after it was placed on the table. "I want the piece with the boat."

"Of course, you do, but you'll serve your guests first, and by then Aunt Steph should get to the boat."

Steph nodded and called out, "It's time to sing to Ian and Brooke!"

Guests, young and not-so-young, gathered to sing a hearty chorus of *Happy Birthday*, and Ian blew out his candles. Brooke's cake was a two-layer confection sans candles.

"Brooke's is lemon," Steph let them know. "You can choose one or have a slice of each." She cut both and placed slices on plates.

Ian and Liz passed out the servings until Ian got his slice with the fishing boat. Dusty, along with a few others, took his picture, looking delighted with his prize slice. Dusty straightened and looked for Kendra. She stood off to the side, her smile not reaching her eyes. He took her a square of Ian's chocolate cake. "I thought you'd want chocolate."

"I'll go back for the lemon next."

He chuckled. He'd nearly forgotten how much she loved sweets, but only indulged on special occasions. "There's plenty."

"Thank you, Dusty."

He shrugged. "It's just cake."

"Not for that. For everything. For coming up to see if I was all right. For being a good father. I've wanted to tell you that for a while. You're a great dad. Ian is fortunate to have you."

His throat tightened. Most parents probably questioned whether or not they were messing up their kids, and he had his moments of doubt, but he'd spent six years knocking himself out to be enough for this child who deserved more. Dusty couldn't do it without his mom, and she often assured him he was doing a good job and had told him the truth about his mistakes when he'd asked. But hearing Kendra say the words meant everything. Saying them had cost her something, something he couldn't even imagine.

She took a bite and still he said nothing.

"Oh, my goodness." She rolled her eyes and took another bite.

And the moment passed.

❦

Piper texted on Sunday, saying she had Monday off. She asked Kendra to spend some time with her and have lunch in Olde Town. After an early class, the rest of Kendra's day was open, so she agreed. She hadn't seen much of the growing trendy area, where stores and restaurants catered to tourists, so she looked forward to doing something with Piper. She needed friends.

"Let's walk along the river before it gets too hot, unless you're super hungry," Piper suggested after they met in a parking area. She looked different in a floral sundress and sandals, with her platinum hair in a messy bun, rather than her usual jeans and ponytail.

"Wow, you look great, and no I'm not starving."

"I don't wear my red shirt and apron every day, you know."

"I didn't realize this area had grown so large."

"It's pretty much all the area east of Chickering Road, between the Willow Drive Bridge and the fairgrounds."

There was Chickering Road East, which bordered the east side of Spencer and Chickering Road South, which ran along the river on the west side of town. The river Piper spoke of was The Gold River, fed from Poudre Lake. If one drove north on Chickering Road they'd head out of town on Highway thirty-four, so she spoke of shopping, artists, restaurants, and museums covering a couple of miles.

"I've seen all the murals on the backs of the buildings from the park," Kendra mentioned as they walked.

Piper dug a wrinkled map out of her cross-shoulder bag and unfolded it. "What would you like to see?

They paused for Kendra to look it over and figure out the walking path. "The Old Stone Church looks interesting. Weavers and Native American Art." She pointed to a spot. "And the Pony Express Station has a historical museum?"

"Okay, and between those two places is the Old Time Soda Shop, so we can have lunch there, unless you don't eat burgers and shakes."

"Oh, I love burgers and shakes."

"Great. We'll just stop anywhere that strikes our fancy."

The Pony Express museum was closest, so they went

there first, enjoyed the displays and exhibits, and then strolled along a path past a weathered-bronze statue of a pony express rider leaning forward over the neck of a galloping full-size horse. Kendra appreciated the details in the young man's face, the folds of his clothing and the horse.

There was a larger-than-life-size statue of a pioneer woman with a baby in her arms and a small boy at her side in the center of a square of shops. The child's head had been rubbed shiny by the touch of thousands of passersby. The soda shop was located on the north of the square. Inside looked like the set of Happy Days with black and white square tiled floor, small round tables on chrome pedestals and red padded chairs with chrome legs. People filled the booths, tables and stools at the counter, but Piper found them a booth that was only then being cleaned off, and they slid into the seats.

Kendra glanced around at families and couples. "Is it always like this?"

"Spring through fall, yes. You can book parties in the winter. Wait till you try the food."

"If it tastes as good as it looks, I'll come back and book a winter party."

Piper laughed.

They ordered and chatted, and their food was served surprisingly quick. The burgers came in paper-lined red plastic baskets and the shakes in stemmed soda glasses with three inches of whipped cream and a cherry.

"I expect to see Richie and Potsie any minute," Kendra said, using her napkin.

"Or Laverne and Shirley. My mom used to watch that."

"They were the best." Neither of them could finish their meals, but Kendra enjoyed every bite she could stuff in. "I'd better not come back here any time soon."

"Would you like coffee?"

"I'd love a cup."

"The jukebox runs non-stop without coins. It's digital music, not records."

"That's seriously cool."

"This is nice." Piper thanked the waitress and sipped her coffee. "I heard something."

Kendra looked at her. Had someone at the birthday party spread gossip about her confrontation with Lacey yesterday? She couldn't think of anyone who would do that. "Go ahead."

"It wasn't anyone being mean. It was just a conversation at Pearls. A couple of people talking. I don't think it's even much of a secret."

"Go on."

"That Lacey Price is Ian's grandmother?"

Kendra nodded. "Yep."

"But you're not his mom."

"Nope."

"And you said you were engaged to him once?"

"Yes."

"So…you're Ian's aunt?"

"I guess I am." Kendra had never connected that relationship in her head before. She nodded. "I guess I am. He doesn't know that, of course."

"So, your sister…?"

"Is his mother. Yes. That's what happened. That's why I left Spencer."

"Wow, Kendra. I knew Dusty had a kid. I mean Liz brings him to the VFW sometimes. But I never heard anything about his mother that I remember."

"I'm surprised you didn't hear about it from someone. Especially after Lacey started seeing Ian as a baby."

"Most of the people I know are customers, so who would have told me?"

Kendra shrugged.

"I don't know Dusty that well but cheating sure doesn't sound like something he'd do."

"It sure doesn't. I didn't suspect anything until he had to tell me. I mean, things were weird, and I couldn't put my finger on it, but then he told me Erica was pregnant and testing had proven he was the father. You can't argue with DNA."

"Did he see the results for sure? It wasn't just her word for it?"

"He got the report the same time she did. And there's no doubt about where Ian got his features."

"What did he have to say about it? I know this is personal. I won't say anything to anyone else."

"Thank you. It's nice to have someone to talk to about it, actually. I never know if people don't know or it's just too awkward." She turned her mug in a circle. "He didn't say anything, and I didn't give him a chance to explain anything. What's to explain? I didn't need details. I know how babies are made. He couldn't deny it, not staring at DNA proof."

"What does he say about it now?"

"I don't give him a chance to say anything. I don't want to talk about it with him. I know he wants to say he's sorry. I know that. I get it. But what good would it do? Sorry can't fix this. I suppose he wants to relieve his conscience."

"And maybe make you understand that he's truly sorry," Piper pointed out.

"So, he gets to feel better?"

Piper shrugged. "Maybe. I don't know." She drummed her fingers on the table a minute and then leaned forward. "As Dr. Phil would say, 'How's that workin' for ya?'"

"Nothing's working for me."

"Well, maybe you need to change your plan of action then."

Kendra studied her new friend's pretty face, fair skin,

gorgeous hair. Her honesty and straightforward conversation were refreshing. Kendra didn't want to act as though she was flipping the tables on her, so she saved personal questions about Piper for another time.

Piper look at her through slightly squinted eyes. "Sorry if I overstepped."

"You didn't." Kendra looked at her hands on the table. "Yesterday I admitted to myself that I didn't have to buy my aunt's house. I don't have to come back here to teach every summer, knowing I'll eventually run into him, into Lacey and Erica. So why did I buy the house? And why do I come back every year? If I really wanted him—wanted the whole thing—out of my life—out of my mind for good…well then I'd move to New York or Chicago or Philadelphia or I'd tour and just travel."

"That's being pretty honest with yourself."

"People live with nightmare situations all the time, I know they do. Children die, people are paralyzed, have to live with a relative gone missing and don't know where they are. Mothers and wives and husbands lose their loved ones to shootings. Those are all horrific things that people are living with. My fiancé cheated on me. Not so big. I need to move past this."

"No, it's a big deal. It's hurtful. It's a shot to your self-confidence. You have to wonder what you did or didn't do, all that."

Kendra tilted her head in acknowledgement.

"By not letting him tell you he's sorry, who are you punishing? Him or yourself?"

"What is there to say? I don't want to forgive him. I didn't get to choose this life. He and Erica took my life and gave me this one. I'm angry."

"You have every right to be."

Kendra spread her fingers on the table. "But I'm trying to

give myself perspective. I'm acknowledging this isn't the worst-case scenario."

"It's the worst for you." Piper pursed her lips a moment as though in thought, then asked, "What's the best-case scenario? You know what you wanted before. You had a plan for your life, and it was all shot to hell. There's no going back. What do you want now?"

Kendra just looked at her, unable to put her thoughts together.

"If you could make it happen right now," she pressed, "leaving the past the same, what would you make happen?"

"Where do you get this stuff?"

"Counseling."

"Seriously?"

"Yes."

Kendra took a deep breath. "Can I have some time to answer that question?"

"Sure. Let's go to the Old Stone Church."

The day spent with Piper had been enjoyable and relaxing, even if somewhat uncomfortable. No one had ever confronted her about her reactions or feelings before, and forcing her to look at herself might be exactly what she needed. Kendra hadn't realized just how much she'd been missing by cutting herself off from having friends. Thankfully, Piper had initiated conversations at Pearls and invited her to that first fish fry, or she'd have missed out on her friendship. The connection she felt surprised her, because her sister had always been a thorn in her side, and she had experienced mostly rivalry and jealousy among professional dancers.

In all the time she'd spent avoiding others, she'd missed meeting good people. The realization surprised her and gave her an unfamiliar sense of expectation. Dusty's sisters were incredible, and she'd enjoyed talking to Brianna. How much had she missed out on by being afraid to feel?

She thought a lot about Piper's question. If she could make it happen right now, leaving the past the same, what would she make happen? Leaving the past the same, of course. She didn't have a time machine. Looking ahead. She would still dance and teach. She would have friends, which she hadn't expected to want. She would read and spend time on the lake. She would have someone to love and to love her. If she could make it happen....

He'd put his number in her phone.

Sitting in her car before going into her class the next morning, she sat looking at the entry in her contacts for five minutes. Finally, she tapped it open and touched the tiny green icon.

One ring. Two.

❧

Dusty's phone vibrated in his pocket on his way out of his office on the mezzanine floor at the lodge. He had a morning head-of-department meeting in fifteen minutes, and this wasn't a good time for an emergency. He glanced toward the meeting room on the other side of the mezzanine. Deke Ward, the head of security, was already heading in with a travel cup of coffee. Dusty shifted his report folder under his arm and slid out his phone. Unknown caller. Everyone who called him was in his contact list, so it wasn't school or a lodge emergency.

"Dustin Cavanaugh."

"Dusty?"

Her voice sluiced over him like warm honey. She'd called him. He couldn't even remember how many years it had been since he'd heard her voice in the phone, but he recognized it with that one word. "Kendra. Are you all right?"

"I'm fine." A moment passed. "I think I'm ready to talk."

Relief washed over him. She would talk to him. His pleasure abruptly faded. Talking would hurt her. It would hurt both of them. That wasn't what he wanted. But he did want things out in the open. "All right. Yes. When? Where?"

Silence stretched while he held his breath. "How about Saturday sometime. Can your mom watch Ian? We could meet…." Her voice trailed off, before she supplied, "At the lake. You know where."

"I know where. What time?"

"Early evening? Seven?"

"I'll ask mom if Ian can stay with her overnight. That way I don't have to wake him up to take him home."

"Where *is* your home?"

"I built a house north by Larkspur Lake. It's about ten minutes from my mom's place."

"Sounds nice."

"It's nice enough. I got a good deal on land, so it's an investment, and I still have more to build on."

"Okay. See you Saturday."

"See you then."

He hung up and realized his heart was beating fast.

He walked forward, then stopped and went back into his office, closing the door. He had to assimilate that life-changing conversation and compartmentalize it so he could go into the other room and do his job.

She'd built a wall between them and had never let him say any of the things he'd needed to say. Even after all this time he didn't know how or what to say, but she was ready, and he could apologize. He would have plenty of time to think about it between now and Saturday, probably too much time. For now, he had people depending on him and responsibilities beyond his personal life.

Dusty took a few deep breaths, collected himself and headed toward the meeting room. After grabbing himself a cup of coffee, he greeted the department heads and took a seat. These meetings lasted about half an hour unless something came up that needed more discussion. Today was that day.

"As we all know the Halloween Ball is scheduled for October thirty-first, just like every year." Deke Ward had been the head of security when Dusty came on board. Rumor had it he'd been a lawman accused and acquitted of murder, and Jakob Spencer had hired him when no one else would. He was all business, with his short-cropped black hair and beard turned mostly white, and intensely loyal to Jakob. The safety of the Spencer family was his responsibility, and he took it seriously. He looked to Dusty.

Dusty quickly flipped through his spreadsheets, discussing reports with the others. "We're on track for all safety inspections the last week of September. HVAC, water treatment, fire safety, alarms, baggage scanners, intercoms, monitors. That gives us time for replacements or repairs as needed." He glanced up. "I need daily property inspection documents from each department today and every day forward. Email them to my office."

Everyone knew the importance the job for which they'd been hired played in the safety of guests, employees and the Spencers. He was proud to work with this elite group of behind-the-scenes experts. Everyone employed at Aspen Gold Lodge had undergone a thorough background and security check to weed out potential problems. They'd signed confidentiality and nondisclosure agreements when they'd accepted these positions.

The meeting ended and Dusty headed back to his office. His assistant had arrived and offered him a cup of coffee, but he declined with a thank you. For the most part, the entire Spencer family, as well as their friends, attended the yearly costume party. Jakob was Dusty's great-uncle on his father's side, and several of the Spencers were second and third cousins, and he'd been to the ball numerous times. Now that he was an employee of the lodge, attending felt like a conflict of interests, but Jakob had always encouraged him to be there. It was actually a good time to catch up with family he didn't see during the rest of the year. Kendra would be back in Denver by then. The thought sunk in his belly like a weight.

But she'd agreed to talk to him. He sat at his desk, checked the time, and opened files that were a blur in front of him. All this time he'd wanted to talk things out with her, needed to apologize. Now he had no idea what he was going to say to her or what difference it would make. All he could do was be encouraged that these lines of communication were opening. Neither of them was the same person they'd been back then. Maybe enough time had passed that repairs could now be made.

It was going to be a long week.

CHAPTER 10

*D*usty had packed a bag with bottles of water, a couple of beers and grabbed a blanket to toss in the back seat of his truck. His mom had assured him they would have fun that evening and Ian would get to bed on time. He headed back to his truck as Crosby was coming around the side of the house.

"Hey," Dusty called to his brother.

"Mom told me Ian was staying over tonight. Big plans?"

"Meeting Kendra to talk."

"Good luck, man."

"Thanks."

"I'm going to teach Ian to play poker and smoke cigars."

"Ha."

"Or maybe he'll teach me about The Wiggles."

"He's way beyond The Wiggles."

"Thank God."

"You'll learn all there is to know about Dinotrux though. And Mom has already opened the LEGO® tote. That was always your favorite."

Crosby groaned. "No those were your favorite. We'll start

a YouTube channel and I'll record him playing practical jokes on Mom."

"And how long will that last until she catches on?"

"Oh, she's gullible. I do it all the time."

"Shut up." Dusty laughed, got in his truck and backed out of the drive.

He oversaw maintenance of the cabins on the northwest edge of the lake that belonged to the lodge, but he never drove farther east anymore. The road was overgrown, but there were still tracks left by young people heading out to park or drink beer undisturbed. Joe had told him the sheriffs occasionally broke up a party, but for the most part the area was secluded.

The sight of her car parked next to a patch of tall weeds made his heart skip. He parked beside it and got out. He picked up a beer bottle a tossed it into the bed of his truck.

He found her sitting on the grassy bank. She'd been smart to wear jeans. She heard him approaching and got to her feet. "Hey."

"Hey. Are the mosquitos biting?"

"Not yet, but I have repellant in my bag."

He nodded.

She gestured to the ground. "Want to sit?"

"Sure." He lowered himself to the grass. "I did bring a blanket for self-preservation."

"We should be okay. Insects aren't bad lately." She sat down, keeping a couple of feet between them. "Did you get Ian taken care of?"

"Yeah. Crosby's there with them. Who knows what they'll watch or talk about?"

"Your mom's there to protect his innocence."

He emitted a laugh. "Right."

They both turned to look out over the lake.

"He's a great kid, Dusty."

"He is."

He didn't mind the comfortable silence for the next few minutes. It was nice simply being with her, knowing he had this time he'd missed for so long.

"Firstly," she said finally. "I want you to know I respect you. I respect that you took responsibility for a brand-new baby without even questioning your decision. You just charged headfirst into being a parent one-hundred-and-fifty percent and gave him everything a child needs."

An unanticipated tug of emotion worked in Dusty's throat, and he swallowed around it. Not taking responsibility had never been a consideration. He had a child. The child's mother didn't want him. Dusty's code of honor and his family dynamic hadn't left him options. "It was the right thing. The only choice."

"For you it was. I know that." She picked up a twig and tossed it toward the water, but it fell short. "The thing was...I didn't have a choice. I was no part of that. Back then I thought you and I were forever...that we had something special...and then you dropped a life-changing bomb on me."

There was no rebuttal. She was finally telling him her story, and he needed to hear it. It might be easier for her to say these things without him looking at her, so she looked out toward the ripples on the lake.

"And with *her*, Dusty. Of all the girls in Spencer, in Colorado—out of all the girls in the freakin' world...with *her*." In his peripheral vision, her fingers clutched the grass beside her hip.

The ultimate betrayal. The weight of shame and confusion was as heavy now as it had been the moment Erica had confronted him about her pregnancy. His actions had cost Kendra so much. Had hurt her. Had changed her. He turned to look at her, but her gaze was on the water.

"I don't know how I'd have felt if it had been someone

else," she said. "I don't know if I'd have been able to listen. To understand. To move past. I don't know, because it *wasn't* someone else." She finally turned to look at him. "And you knew me. You knew all my deepest secrets…about my family and how I felt about her."

The storm in her eyes broke his heart, and he was responsible.

"And you were seeing her."

"I wasn't seeing her." He stopped her there. "Everything you said is true. I knew how you felt about her, and I would never have deliberately done that to you. My life was ruined too, because I loved you. I loved you so much that I have never moved on."

"So, your excuse is you were drunk."

"I don't have an excuse." He'd tried to explain that night to her, but she hadn't been willing to listen. "I only have an explanation, which doesn't excuse me. I came to a party out here during Spring break. There was a lot of drinking going on, and I was doing more than my fair share. I admit that. The truth is I don't remember what happened. There's a point where the night just disappeared. I remember sitting in the back of my pickup with Glen, Trevor, a few of the guys, and the next thing I remembered, I was waking up on Anthony Burnham's floor. He and Glen had hauled me to his house because I was passed out."

She studied his face, her expression unrevealing. But she was listening. Taking in his words.

"The guys told me I was wrecked. They found me stumbling and falling and stopped me from diving into the freezing cold lake. I don't remember any of that."

"Nothing."

"Nothing. Weeks later when Erica came to the house and asked to talk to me, I thought something had happened to you, so I let her in. She handed me a DNA kit and told me she needed a test. I told her she was nuts, but my mom had overheard, and she thought I should do the test just to get Erica off my back. I didn't tell you because I didn't want to freak you out. I thought the test would show she was trying to pull a fast one, and I'd just move on."

"But it didn't."

"The results were mailed directly to me, proving there was ninety-nine-point nine percent certainty I was her child's biological father. I grilled Anthony mercilessly about who he saw me with, what I might have done, what he saw me drink or if I took anything. No one had seen me with her.

"I didn't go to class for a week. I barely ate or slept. I knew right then that my life was irreversibly changed. I thought about fighting the test. I thought someone had mixed up results or something. I even suspected that maybe Erica had forged paperwork or results somehow. Then she showed me a couple of pictures on her phone. They were dark, but they were pictures of me with her that night. I knew then that if I did something to try to prove myself not this child's father—when everything pointed to the fact that I was—he would one day learn that."

She nodded and looked away.

"I told her I'd pay for her medical care if she'd have the baby and give it to me."

"I'm sure she wanted more."

He nodded. "My parents helped me out."

Across the water came the *do weep do weep* of the wood ducks. A familiar sound more akin to pleasant summer memories with Kendra than the sordid story he was revealing now.

Kendra rested her elbows on her knees and brushed her bare arms with her palms. "Of course, he's yours. That had to have been obvious when he was born."

"And more so every day."

"I knew you didn't feel anything for her."

"Of course not."

"She never asked you to marry her? She never tried to come on to you after that?"

"Never. I've only ever glimpsed her in town." He shifted so he was facing her. "I am responsible for my actions. I should never have been in that position. I should never have had so much to drink that I did something so unforgiveable and stupid. I can't deny it happened because there is living evidence. I get that it's hard to believe I can't remember. Obviously, I did what she claims, so I must be that kind of a person."

Her dark gaze moved over his face. There was nothing he regretted more than hurting her. "You've never lied to me Dusty. You may have kept this to yourself for a couple of weeks until the test results came in, but you didn't lie to me. I believe you."

At those words his whole body reacted, his heart, the blood pulsing through his veins, his vision. He blinked and inhaled. After years of holding this inside, admitting what happened to her and knowing she believed him removed a weight from his heart. Nothing had changed, but she'd given him the chance to explain.

He looked away because the pain in her eyes was more than he could bear. A fish jumped in the water with a plop and a circle of ripples. The sun was lowering, reflecting oranges, yellows and purples on the shining surface of the lake. If he never had another chance after this, he wanted to say all the things he'd never said.

"I know how much this hurt you. I couldn't fix it then, and I can't fix it now. I get that these words aren't worth a steaming pile of crap…." He turned toward her, studied her profile in the glow of evening light. The sight of her still made his heart beat fast, stole his breath. "But, Kendra, I'm sorry. I'm not only sorry it happened and that the act came to light, and our lives were changed…I'm sorry I let it happen in the first place. I'm sorry I was there in that place that night. I'm so sorry I hurt you."

She nodded. "Okay."

Okay. She'd let him say it. She didn't have to forgive him. But she believed him.

"I have never stopped loving you, Kendra. Not for a moment. I've lived every day and night wanting you, thinking about what we had, the plans we made. I don't expect I could ever make it up to you, but I promise I'll try if you let me."

She turned her head to look at him.

Kendra believed her heart had turned to stone a long time ago. Dusty's words showed her differently, because everything in her chest ached again. She believed that he was sorry. And she believed he had no memory of Ian's conception. She even believed he loved her. What she wasn't sure of was whether or not either of them could put the past behind them.

She leaned toward him and rested her palm along his jaw, testing the warmth of his skin, the texture, the familiarity. She didn't want to be the kind of person who couldn't forgive, but she didn't know if she had that much strength. She missed him. She loved him. Still. Always. Even in this light, his blue gaze revealed sincerity, regret…desire, and cut through her sensibilities.

He raised a hand to her shoulder, barely applying pressure to draw her closer. She folded into his arms, remembering how he'd held her and comforted her in the bathroom at Ian's party. He'd been her rock for all the days of her formative years and into college. During high school, she'd worked at the library, and he'd picked her up each night after her shift and driven her home. Sometimes they'd stopped for a burger or ice cream, sometimes they'd stopped simply to talk. He'd always been her best friend. She'd missed him unbearably.

Wrapping her arm around his neck, she opened her other hand to cup his jaw, and initiated a kiss that started out tentative…and within minutes went right to all-consuming need. They toppled over onto the grass and he covered her face and neck with kisses that shot tingles down her shoulders and arms, along her thighs.

He stroked her back and sides through her shirt, and she clung to him as though she couldn't get close enough. She'd missed this. She'd missed him.

Around the sighs of their combined breaths, he said, "I have a blanket in the truck."

She moved her head back and bracketed his face. "We're grown-ass adults now. I have a house. Privacy. A comfortable bed. Really comfortable."

"You won't change your mind by the time we get there, driving separate cars?"

"I won't change my mind."

He kissed her again, hard and with a promise. "Then let's go."

❧

At the soft breathing beside her and the delightful heat along her side, Kendra opened her eyes. Early morning light peeked through her bedroom curtains. She turned her head. Dusty lay on his stomach, his wavy hair mussed, his muscled shoulders bare, one arm under his cheek. She took a mental picture for later. Closed her eyes to remember it—and the previous night.

No one who didn't love a woman could treat her with as much tenderness and adoration as Dusty had treated her.

She didn't have much experience with others to compare it to, but last night had been a reunion of lovers. It had been like college days when he'd come home for the weekends and they'd been unable to keep their hands off each other. Their lovemaking had been exciting and new, yet familiar and relaxed all at the same time. She'd been dying of thirst and he was fresh spring water.

She didn't resist the urge to turn toward him and stroke the warm skin of his muscled shoulders. His hair was thick and silky between her fingers.

He raised his head to peer at her over his bicep. "How can you be so pretty in the morning?"

"I was wondering the same thing."

He rolled to his side to face her, deliberately tugging the sheet and drawing her closer. "I'm not pretty."

"You're pretty sexy." She leaned in and kissed his cheeks, his eyelids, his nose.

Unsatisfied with those kisses, he raised his chin and captured her lips with his. "I guess you've always fallen victim to my sexy."

"Not always. You were dorky in fifth grade."

"You didn't mind."

"I stuck it out. By seventh grade you were cute enough."

"Oh really."

"Freshman year, though…." She wrapped her fingers around his upper arm. When you started growing these?"

"That did it for you, huh?" He raised his arm and flexed the bicep for her.

"Pretty much." She grinned, gave him another kiss and rolled over on her back. "Why did you invite me to your place when we were kids? I didn't go at first because I thought you felt sorry for me."

"I didn't feel sorry for you. I admired you."

"Get serious."

"I am. You had this gutsy attitude that filled a space. Some of the kids thought you were stuck up. You entered a room like you owned it. Sat by yourself all confident like. You weren't giggly or silly like the other girls. You didn't try to make anybody like you. It was like you didn't care what anyone thought, and you weren't going to waste your time wondering."

"I had crap to wear, Dusty. I cared plenty. Those girls were petty and mean."

"I never noticed what you wore. I noticed your hair, your eyes, the way you walked and carried yourself—chin up, shoulders back."

"I was a dancer."

"You were a beast."

They looked into each other's eyes for a long moment.

He reached for her hand and their fingers twined.

"I saw you dance in Philadelphia," he said finally.

His statement threw her off guard. "When was that?"

He told her the year, the date, the program. "I was there for business, but I checked ahead and bought tickets. I could hardly breathe during your every performance. You were incredible. You are incredible. I like remembering."

Hot tears welled in her eyes. She'd read numerous reviews, been complimented a hundred times, but none of that praise touched her as deeply as Dusty's. Dance was the part of her life that had saved her—as a child and as an adult. She'd learned discipline. She'd earned every spot in those troupes, every accolade. Performing had filled an empty place within her. Teaching had given her an outlet for her passion and supplied necessary human connection. Dance had never let her down.

"It's not creepy, is it? I just wanted to see you."

"It's not creepy." She turned and looked at him. "Tell me about when you first got Ian. What was that like?"

"I wanted to finish college, so I transferred closer to home before he was born. We put a crib in my old room and lived there until I graduated. I couldn't have studied or gotten to classes otherwise. Mom, the twins and Crosby all helped take care of him. Mom said he was an easy baby. I didn't call middle of the night bottles, teething or upset stomachs and getting puked on easy, but apparently all that was normal."

"And Lacey? Where did she fit in back then?"

"She asked to see him soon after he was born. My folks and I talked about it, and we didn't think it was right to keep Ian from a grandparent who wanted to be part of his life. She came over on Sunday evenings and spent time with him. After I built my house and moved out, things had been going well, so those visits continued at my place and when he was old enough, I started leaving him at her house."

"Only on her day off."

"Only Sunday evenings. If I have a conference out of town, Mom keeps him. Lacey is one more person who loves him. I believe she does. She's kept the conditions of our agreement in order to see him."

He got up and went into the bathroom and she pulled on a short cotton robe. When he came out, they looked at each other a moment before he asked, "Plans for today?"

"I usually bake on Sundays."

"How about we take the boat out this morning? Maybe swim."

"Now?"

"After a cup of coffee."

She couldn't remember the last time she'd swam in the lake. They'd done it all the time when they were kids. "Okay." She pulled open a drawer and found her swimsuit. She turned to him. "What will you swim in?"

"The lake."

"You know what I mean."

"I'll just swim in my sexy, unless that bothers you."

She grinned and headed for the bathroom. "I'll be down in a couple of minutes. "Pods are in the cupboard left of the sink. You'll have to add fresh water."

"Pods?"

"For the coffee maker?"

"Okay, gotcha. I know how. I've got one at the office."

A few minutes later, with shorts over her suit, she followed the scent of coffee to the kitchen. "Are you hungry?"

Wearing only his jeans, he handed her a mug. "I'm always hungry."

She took a sip before setting down her coffee and pulling ingredients from the fridge. "Eggs, cheese, yogurt and cantaloupe. Will that hold you?"

"If you make it four eggs."

"I have bread in the freezer too. You can have toast."

After eating and quickly cleaning up, she grabbed water bottles and towels while Dusty headed for the boathouse. She steered the boat out onto the lake. "Will your mom be wondering where you are this morning?"

"No, she'll be taking Ian to church. I'll be there for dinner this afternoon. You're always welcome."

She glanced around. "This look like a good spot."

In reply, Dusty stripped off his jeans and dove into the water. She removed her shorts and followed. Though the morning was warm, the water was shockingly cold. She came up gasping. "I f-forgot how cold it is!"

They dog paddled, floated on their backs and then Kendra took a good long swim for exercise and returned out of breath. Dusty, wrapped in a pink towel, helped her into the boat, draped her with another, and rubbed her arms through the thick terrycloth to warm her. "The sun will heat you up."

"Forget the sun, I want a hot shower and to wash this fish water out of my hair. Get me home."

She beat him to the shower, while inside the boathouse he hoisted the boat out of the water and locked up.

"You did all that dressed in a pink towel?" she asked when he found her getting dressed.

"Worried about my masculinity?"

"Not in the least."

He showered and convinced her to join the family for dinner.

❧

Kendra had taken pastries from her freezer to contribute to the meal. Dusty appreciated how his family had welcomed her back into the fold, and even his grandmother had a soft spot for her. Ian had found him the minute he entered the house and vaulted into his arms. Wearing shorts and a t-shirt, Ian smelled like soap and his mother's line-dried sheets. He couldn't get enough of this kid.

After the meal, the family gathered outdoors for games, but the sun was blistering hot and the humidity high, so they filtered back into the house and watched a movie. Kyle and Avery weren't there because there was a birthday party at Colette's parents, so Chloe and Ian played Go Fish until Chloe wanted to be on her phone. Kendra took her place and searched for pairs of angler fish and shrimp until Dusty saved her and put on a kids' movie. Ian fell asleep for an hour.

Kendra helped Steph put out leftovers and a cheese tray for a light supper, and by the time they'd eaten, it was time to take Ian to Lacey's.

"Riding along?" Dusty asked. "I'll bring you back here for your car." They had driven separately.

She joined him once again as they drove along Forest Lake Drive. There was a car parked in Lacey's driveway when Dusty pulled his truck to a stop behind it. Kendra's sharp intake of breath alerted him to her sudden anxiety.

She pushed her sunglasses up on her head and looked at him, eyes wide.

He leaned his head to the side and asked a question with his eyes.

"It's *her*." Her whisper was barely audible.

He frowned. *Who?*

Kendra opened her door, which she had deliberately not done last time.

Dusty got out and helped Ian unbuckle and lifted him down.

Kendra was halfway to the house, and he half-ran to catch up. Ian ran ahead and up the porch stairs.

The door opened and Lacey stepped outside, immediately showing surprise as Kendra barreled toward her. "Well, this is unexpected."

"What's she doing here?"

"I don't know that that's any of your business."

"I'm making it my business. What is she doing here?"

"Hi, Grammy," Ian said cheerfully.

Lacey diverted her attention and bent to give him a hug. "Hello there, sweet boy."

"Keep him out here," she said to Lacey and took a step toward the door.

"Don't go startin' trouble."

Kendra ignored her and went inside. Dusty gave Lacey a quick glance and hurried in after.

Erica got up from a chair at a table in the sparse dining room that was open to the living area. Her face showed no surprise at seeing her sister.

"What is this, Erica?"

"This is still my mom's house, and I can come here whenever I like. You're the one barging in."

"You need to leave now."

Erica stood and stepped closer. "Always the prima donna, aren't you? Better than the rest of us. New car. Two places to live. I probably don't make enough in a week to buy these sunglasses." She reached up and plucked them from Kendra's head. "You still don't get to tell me what to do."

Kendra snatched back her sunglasses. "The way I understand it, you signed away your rights to Dusty's child a long time ago."

"I got Ian a present for his birthday. I just wanted to see him. That's not a crime. I haven't come to kidnap him."

Dusty noticed the package on the table. He didn't like Erica showing up here anymore than Kendra did, but their tempers concerned him. He didn't want Ian caught in the middle of something ugly. "Maybe I should take him and go."

"Yes," Kendra said.

"No," Lacey said from the doorway. "Aunt Erica brought a gift for Ian's birthday, so he can stay. I'll be watching him. We'll all be just fine."

Ian stepped around her and spotted Erica and the gift on the table. "Is that really for me?"

Dusty's heart sank, and he let his glance bounce off Kendra's distressed expression. He couldn't let this get out of hand or allow anyone to say something detrimental. "Yes, it's for you," he answered in the most normal voice he could muster. "Why don't you come see what it is?"

Ian ran toward the dining room table.

"I'll stay and handle this." He reached into his front pocket, withdrew his keys, and extended them toward Kendra. "Go ahead and take my truck back to the house. You can send someone back for me later."

The hurt and mistrust in her eyes gnawed at his gut all

over again. He couldn't allow a confrontation in front of Ian. Someone would say something they shouldn't. He needed to stay here and make sure that didn't happen. And obviously Kendra couldn't be here.

Her stormy gray-green gaze was a tempest. She didn't look at anyone but him. Her arm raised stiffly. She grabbed the keys and walked toward the door, her back straight, her head high, the way she always faced adversity.

Kendra didn't know what she was feeling. Mad. Hurt. Blindsided. Again.

Lacey followed her out, closing the door behind her. "She's his mother, Kendra," she said softly. "She should be allowed to see her child and know he's okay."

Kendra kept moving forward.

"She's really changed this time. It's not always all about you, you know."

She didn't stop. Without a word, Kendra got into the truck, adjusted the electric seat and backed out of the driveway. Leaving Ian and Dusty there inside that house with Erica. And Lacey.

Her hands trembled on the steering wheel as she drove through Spencer and headed north. She pulled into Liz Cavanaugh's driveway, stuck Dusty's keys behind the visor, grabbed her purse and got into her car.

What had she expected? That Erica and Lacey would suddenly disappear? Or decide to leave the Cavanaughs in peace? She did not live in a fantasy world. Dusty was bound to them for life.

❧

Dusty watched Ian open the package as Lacey and Erica encouraged him. Anger simmered beneath the calm exterior he worked to project.

"Look, Dad!" Ian had unwrapped a huge water gun. "This is going to be so much fun! Isn't it great?" Lacey used a pair of scissors to cut the toy from the packaging.

"Can I talk to you for a minute?" he asked Erica.

Her expression stiffened, but she walked into the other room with him.

"You blindsiding me like this is not going to happen again. You have no legal right to see him. You signed away all parental privileges, or have you forgotten?"

"I can be his aunt or something."

"I'm not going to start lying to him, and no decent parent would. You thinking it's convenient to lie only proves how ill-equipped you are to have a relationship with him."

"Listen to you, all full of yourself because you have your big family with your fancy houses and your new trucks. You're not better than we are because you have money."

"This is not going to happen again, do you understand me? I can take you back to court and get a restraining order against you."

"Again, with your money for lawyers, so you can get whatever you want. You're going to be the one lying to him if you let him think his mother never wanted to see him. I could tell him right now so you can't lie to him anymore."

He stared at her, angrier and more disgusted than he'd ever been in his life. How Kendra could be related to these two women was beyond comprehension.

"Let me have just this little bit of time," she whispered. "And I'll stay quiet."

"What kind of vile person are you?" Dusty asked. "You're using a child for manipulation."

"Then I guess you're the one who has the problem with the truth. So shut the hell up."

Dusty took a deep breath. He had to control himself and

the situation until he could get Ian out of there. "You have as long as it takes for me to get a ride here."

He took his phone out of his pocket and she walked back to the dining room. "You're going to have fun with that, aren't you?" she said to Ian.

◈

Kendra stripped the bed and washed sheets and towels, removing all evidence of the previous night. She cleaned the bathroom, climbed the stairs and flipped on the overhead strings of Edison lights in her studio, which sent a glow across the shiny hardwood floor. She didn't turn on music but slid to sit on the floor in the quiet.

An hour passed like that. In the stillness of the dark house, the ratcheting sound of the old-fashion crank door-bell was loud. She knew who it was and ignored the sound, though it repeated several times.

She thought he'd given up, but then she heard a sound like the front door opening. Oh man, he knew where the key was.

"Kendra?" he called. "I know you're here."

She didn't reply, but her heart hammered.

"Kendra?" he called again, his voice fading in and out as his footsteps sounded from room to room. Finally, the stairs creaked. "Are you up there?"

"Don't come up here," she called. "I didn't give you permission to use that key."

"I want to talk to you. I have to figure out how to fix this."

"I don't want to talk to you. There's nothing you can say to change anything."

"Can we just talk?"

"We've said it all. Leave the key on the table and go."

"Kendra—"

"If you don't leave, I'll call Joe," she threatened. "He's a minute away."

"He's my brother."

"He's a sheriff. I'll tell him you're frightening me."

"You're not afraid of me."

"How do you know how I feel? I'm really uncomfortable that you came into my house when I didn't want you to. That's pretty stalkerish."

"Kendra, we spent the whole night together last night."

"And then you let her see Ian." She caught herself arguing with him. "But that has nothing to do with me. I have nothing to say about him, just as I had nothing to say about anything involving your son. It's not my concern—but I don't have to stick around to watch. You do whatever you want. When my class is finished, I'm out of here. Out of Spencer and out of your lives."

The stairs creaked.

"Do not come up here. Leave now. I'm not bluffing. Go."

A pause and he headed down the stairs. A minute later, the front door closed.

This nightmare wouldn't end. It couldn't. She needed to wake up and move on.

CHAPTER 11

The next Friday evening she met Piper at the VFW for the fish fry. They'd been texting and she'd told Piper that she'd heard Dusty out, but that she couldn't be with him because of Erica.

"I get it," Piper said, sipping her beer. "She's right here in your face. You can't ignore her." She ran her fingertip through the condensation on her glass. "Do you see where he's coming from, though? That's she's Ian's mom?"

"I'm able to look at the situation through Ian's eyes. He's a child who knows his mother didn't want him. But they're not telling him any of that, of course. He doesn't know who she is. The visit was for Erica's benefit, because she wanted to see him. And I can guarantee it won't be the last time, especially now that she's seen how much I don't like her coming around him."

"What was it like growing up with her?"

"Like you can imagine. She was always mean. Always selfish. She certainly never held any affection for me. Junior high and high school were the worst. You probably remember her."

Piper nodded. "She had a pretty bad rep."

"And because my sister screwed everybody, then of course I must be that kind of girl too. The Cavanaughs befriending me helped though. They were respected, and Joe and Dusty were like protective big brothers. Liz even took me for haircuts and bought me some clothes."

"They're great."

"Yeah." Kendra picked at her fish. "But being around their family pointed out what I didn't have. Sam was an amazing guy. He spent time with each of his kids, so they all felt special."

"I remember seeing him with Liz. They seemed really happy."

Kendra nodded. "They set a high bar for their children, for sure."

"Is this girl talk or can a fella get a minute too?" Jonas stood beside the table, dressed in a flannel shirt, though it was still August. He wore an inquiring smile.

"Yes, of course. You're one of our favorite fellas," Piper told him. She scooted over, moving her food and drink.

"You're our *only* favorite fella at the moment," Kendra added.

"Uh oh. Man trouble." He settled onto the padded bench. "I have plenty of tomatoes and peppers if you want to come over and get a basket or two," he told her. "I still plant as many as I did when my Rebecca used to can them. I can't seem to just start a few."

"I'd love to come get some," she replied. "And I'll pick out some onions at the farmer's market and make you a batch of salsa."

"Sounds good. Rebecca always made corn relish too," he told her.

Kendra leaned forward. "Did you catch these delicious fish?"

"A lot of 'em. They were big 'uns today." He nodded and glanced aside before looking back at her. "I see you're not wearing your ring yet."

Kendra exchanged a look with Piper. "No. I won't be wearing that ring."

"Shame."

She pursed her lips and took a drink.

"Shame you two can't work it out while you still have so many years ahead of you."

"Things happen," she said.

"I'd give anything to have more time with Rebecca. Jeeter and Hamm said I'd find someone and marry again." He shook his head. "I knew I wouldn't. She was the one and only. That's a rare thing."

"My grandpa thinks that about my grandma, too," Piper said. "He always says, life wasn't perfect, but there was never anything better than being with her."

Loydell approached their table. "Just found out there's some big event going on in Olde Town, and the Wild Card is pretty empty tonight. Some of us are going to head over for some pool and dancing. Why don't you girls join us? You want to come along Jonas? I'll give you a lift."

"No, thanks. Jeeter wants to play checkers."

"Let's go," Piper said. "Friday night at the Wild Card without all the tourists who find their way in sounds great. They have a band."

Kendra hesitated a little too long.

"You think you'll see your mom."

She nodded.

"If she's working, she'll be on the new side, not the side where the band is. Come on. You have a right to have some fun."

After the week she'd had, a night out did sound like fun. "Okay. Let's go."

Half an hour later, she and Piper pulled into the parking lot behind the Wild Card Saloon that faced Brook Park. The music greeted them before they approached a courtyard strung with lights between two buildings. Tables and chairs filled the space between the two buildings.

"Have you been here before?"

Kendra shook her head. "First time."

"The owner bought out the hardware store and added onto his business. That side's the sports bar with games on all the screens. Your mom is on that side on weekends. The band is in the original building over here." She led the way past tables with Coors umbrellas and people eating and drinking to enter the noisy saloon.

Peanut shells crunched underfoot as Piper led them to an immense glossy wood bar with intricate filigree curved along the front where the wood rolled under. Behind the bar was an obviously old mirror flanked by a framed daguerreotype of a couple unidentifiable people and vintage metal advertising signs.

"Okay to sit here?" Piper asked.

"Sure." They perched on stools and it was only a few seconds before a mature man with long gray-streaked black hair tied back came to get their orders. He was obviously Native American, his dark skin weathered.

"Hello, young Piper," he said.

"Hi, Ace. This is my friend, Kendra."

"Welcome, Kendra. What can I get for you young ladies?"

"Seems I remember you're pretty good at margaritas," Piper answered with a smile. "That's my choice."

"I'll have the same," Kendra told him. She rubbed the surface of the bar. "This is amazing wood. It seems to glow."

"My father bought this place from a Scotsman who brought the piece here after the turn of the century," Ace replied. "There are several stories about the fellow and what went on here, but I don't know how many of them are true. What I do know is that this wood takes a lot of upkeep. I'll be right back with your drinks."

The band was playing *This is How We Roll*. Country wasn't Kendra's first choice in music, but she liked a lot of it and was familiar with the fun, easy-to-dance-to genre.

Others from the VFW filtered in, including Loydell, who was on the dance floor in minutes. *'When the world turns ugly, I just turn and look at you, baby. This is how we roll. This is how we roll, baby.'*

Piper laughed and leaned into Kendra. "Mild-mannered postal worker by day. Wild and crazy party girl at night."

"And probably not an Elvis tune in the set."

They laughed.

Ace refilled their drinks, and after a couple more songs they were on the dance floor too.

News had spread that traffic had been light because of the event in Olde Town and others came in to enjoy the night with locals only. Kendra danced with Jackson Samuels and even with Crosby when he showed up with Brianna. She introduced Piper to Brianna, and the three of them sat out a dance and talked about light-hearted subjects. Matt Chandler showed up, along with Spencer's tall, fair-haired family practitioner, Gabe Ewing.

"Anyone want to get something to eat with me?" Brianna asked. "I'm a lightweight."

"Sure, I will," Kendra told her.

Piper joined them and they ordered burgers and fries and sat in the courtyard. The mountain air had cooled down the evening temperature. Piper collapsed the umbrella so they could see the sky. "This air feels great."

"These are the best fries ever," Brianna added.

Kendra finished a bite of her burger. "This whole evening

feels really good. I didn't know there were so many nice people in Spencer."

"The drinks don't hurt," Piper said.

"No really. I only had bad memories of Spencer. Grade school and junior high were nightmares."

"Why?" Brianna asked. "If it's okay that I ask."

"You can ask. Because my mom was the town slut and my sister the junior town slut. Plus, a whole lot more I won't go into."

"I'm sorry. That sounds terrible."

"It was. They haven't changed. When my class at Holling ends in a couple weeks, I'm heading back to Denver."

"What about Dusty? I thought you two were…I don't know. A thing?"

"We were a thing. But it's not going to work out."

Brianna wiped her fingers on her napkin. "Does this have something to do with Ian?"

Kendra nodded. "My sister has inserted herself into the picture, and I'm not sticking around for it."

Crosby joined them and set a basket of chips and salsa on the table, before pulling over a chair and setting down his beer. He glanced at their faces. "Am I good to sit here?"

"You're good," Kendra told him. "How are the nachos?"

He pushed the cardboard tray toward her, and she tried one. "I've never eaten as much in my life as I've eaten since I've been here this summer. Between your mother, the fish fries and local delights, I'm going to bust out of my leotards."

"You forgot your passion for rhubarb everything," he pointed out.

She jabbed a tortilla chip toward him, saying, "That too."

They both laughed, and she covered her mouth.

Brianna and Piper were having a conversation and trying to remember the name of a local band they liked. Crosby leaned toward her. "I haven't seen my brother as happy in years as he's been since you've been here."

She used her napkin and took a sip of her drink. "We're not even talking right now."

He turned his glass in a circle on the tabletop. "I get it. Nobody blames you. If you ask me, you've got bigger *cojones* than anyone I know. Spending summers here you confront your worst nightmares and stare them down."

"No, I ran."

"No, you lived your best life in spite of the bull. You made something of yourself and you showed everyone what you're made of. Then you come back here every summer and enjoy life at the lake like a boss."

Kendra absorbed his words, watched him eat a couple of cheese-laden chips. He was every bit as handsome as Dusty. His hair was darker, and he had hazel-brown eyes like Joe's. "That's really how you see me?"

He grinned at her. "That's really who you are."

"I'm leaving when my class is finished."

"You have to do what's right for you."

"Are you doing what's right for you?"

"My sisters think I should get out of Mom's house. They say she doesn't need me anymore. But my mom and I are getting along just fine. Mom and I have talked about it, and we're good with the arrangement. I handle all the lawn care and home repairs. We share groceries. It's not like we spend every minute together. She has her life. I have mine, work and school. We see each other at the house. I eat her cooking. It works."

"I think it's nice you have each other." She glanced at Brianna, still talking to Piper. "I like her. Is that getting serious?"

He shook his head. "Nah. I like her too, but that's all it is."

Kendra grinned.

Piper threw their trash in a nearby receptacle and returned. "Sounds like the band is back from their break. Let's go dance."

Kendra joined them.

❖

A few students were already waiting on chairs in the hallway for their scheduled appointments. Today Kendra was showing them their videos from the first class and comparing them to performances she'd recorded earlier this week. She always did this appraisal in private sessions, so as not to create a competitive or uncomfortable situation between the young dancers. Those who chose to move forward with careers in dance would discover the cutthroat rivalry soon enough, without experiencing it among their friends.

Each girl had improved, but none as dramatically as Chloe. Chloe had thrown herself into practice with a determination that outweighed all lack of experience.

"This was a good performance," she told the girl about the first time she'd danced for Kendra. "But this." She clicked on the file with the recent video recording, and it started playing. "This is the most improvement I've ever witnessed in a student." She narrated her thoughts on the routine and then went back through points again. "Your movements are precise and yet emotional, which isn't an easy thing to portray. The height you get in those jumps impresses me because you make them look effortless. It takes strength and concentration, but you make each one graceful. You are a high-energy dancer. You take instruction and you learn choreography quickly."

She shut it off and looked at Chloe, who wiped away tears. "Honey, why are you crying?"

Chloe let out a little sob and swiped her face with her palms. "Because I want so badly to be good."

Kendra had known Chloe since she was a little girl, so she didn't consider it improper to wrap her arms around her. "You're better than good. You're great. You and I are going to talk to your dad about summer camp academy. I know him well enough to know he won't let his little girl go to New York alone, so I'm willing to chaperone you next summer. Be your coach for those eight weeks."

Chloe burst into full-fledged tears against Kendra's shoulder.

"Are you happy?" she asked.

Chloe nodded.

Kendra laughed. "Okay, put on a smile then. I have more students to evaluate. I'll call him and we'll talk, okay?"

"Okay. You don't know how much this means to me."

"I think I do. And that's why I want to do it. Send in Becca, will you, please?"

She'd never had a student with as much potential as this one, and it was a rare privilege to be part of her training. She was every bit as excited about working with Chloe as Chloe was about developing her talent.

She finished her student sessions and afterward called Joe's cell phone from her car in the parking lot.

"Hey, Kendra," he answered.

"Hi, Joe. Are you at work?"

"I am, but I have a minute. What can I do for you?"

"I want to talk to you about Chloe?"

"Is she all right?"

"She's better than all right." She proceeded to tell him her assessment of his daughter's skills and what she proposed for her the following summer. "She has a gift, Joe. And she works incredibly hard. I think she could go far."

He was silent a long while, and finally he said, "This is hard for me. She's all I have."

"I don't want to take her away from you. She doesn't want to leave you. She just wants to dance. I understand her passion. Dance fulfils something inside of me. I think it does for her too. I know she still has high school to finish and you'd like her to go to college, but I was able to do both. She could too."

"I trust you have her best interests at heart."

"I do."

"And I don't want to stand in the way of her doing something she loves like this. If you can make the arrangements, I can swing the money."

"She may be able to qualify for a scholarship. I'll send the academy her video, and a letter of recommendation. We'll see how that goes. If they call her for an interview, it's pretty much a sure thing."

"Okay. Thank you. You've been good for her. She has my mom, of course, and I'm thankful for that, but she's missing a woman like you to take an interest in her."

"I'm honored to be able to help her. I'll call you when I have more information."

She hung up and closed her eyes. She'd been excited from the moment she'd seen Chloe perform, recognized her drive and ability. All it had taken was some direction and work on technique to prove she'd been right to get her hopes up about the girl's talent. At least she'd be able to end her summer on this high note. Everything else might have tanked, but her classes had been worth every minute.

❀

She spent several days working off burgers, fries, margaritas and rhubarb scones. She'd taken a job doing choreography for an off-Broadway play in the fall, and she wanted to impress the producers and prove she was worth her salary. Doing so, meant performing her routines in the preliminaries.

She had motored across the lake and brought home tomatoes and peppers from Jonas's abundant garden. Now her bright-colored jars of salsa were labeled, lined up and stacked on the counters. She stared at them, finally packing a box and loading it in the car. She took a couple to Joe and had him sign Chloe's application. She had lunch at Pearl's and left a jar with Piper. She figured it would be safe to leave a few at Liz's during the day, so she rang the bell.

"Come on in!" Liz wiped her hands on a towel and opened the door for her.

"I brought you some of my salsa."

"That's so kind of you. I'm glad to see you."

"I'll be leaving soon, and I didn't want to go without having a chance to thank you for everything this summer. You've always made me feel like part of your family, and I'm thankful."

"You are part of our family. I just wish things could have worked out differently."

Kendra shook her head. "I don't know how."

"I don't know either." She took the jars and carried them into her kitchen. "Can I get you a glass of lemonade?"

"That sounds good." She sat on a stool at the island. "Did Dusty tell you what happened?"

"He did."

"I don't want to forgive Erica. Maybe I'm broken or hard-hearted or there's something inherently wrong with me, but that's how I feel. It makes me sick to think of Ian being anywhere near her—same goes for Lacey for that matter."

"Your feelings are completely justifiable. You know I love

that boy like he's my own. I've helped take care of him since he was born."

"I know."

"I don't want Erica around him either. Dusty has an appointment for legal counsel later in the week. We don't know what can be done. He told Lacey she can't see Ian again until he gets advice about keeping Erica away from him. No one wants to be the one who kept a child's mother or grandmother from him. Just ask Joe. He'd give anything to have had his wife show an interest in Chloe. But Dusty has to protect Ian. This is so hard for Dusty." Liz straightened her shoulders. "There's going to come a point when we have to tell him the truth, but he's so young."

Liz had a lot of family things going on. "You have your hands full with your own kids," Kendra told her. "You don't need me adding to your list of concerns."

She moved to get up, but Liz put a hand on her shoulder.

"Here's your lemonade." Liz sat down next to her. "Dusty didn't even ask you to forgive him, did he?"

Kendra thought back over everything he'd said. "He said he was sorry more than once."

"But did he ask you to forgive him?"

She considered. "No."

"Because he doesn't think he deserves forgiveness. He took responsibility. He took blame. He shouldered it. And he did what he knew he needed to do. He's sorry. He blames himself."

Kendra rested an elbow on the counter and made a helpless gesture with her hand. "I knew before he said it that an apology would never fix this. I didn't want to let him say it because...I guess some mean-spirited part of me wanted to deny him some sort of pardon by having spoken it—as though the words absolved him somehow."

"You're not mean-spirited."

"I must be."

"No one who has been hurt as much as you have walks themselves right back into a situation where it can happen again."

"But I did! I came here. I saw him. I fell in love with him all over again, even though I knew it was impossible for us to be together. I broke my own heart this time. Not Dusty. Not Erica or my mother. Me."

Liz put her arm around Kendra and drew her head to touch hers. "I wish I could fix this for both of you. I wish I had something wise and profound to say. All I know is that life isn't fair. But somehow love finds a way."

Kendra didn't buy into that. "Not this time it doesn't."

Liz gave her a final hug and released her. "You're always welcome here, you know."

"I do know. Maybe Christmas this year. I usually take a trip somewhere, just to get away."

"We'd love to have you for Christmas."

"I'll have my big girl pants back on by then."

"I have no doubt you will."

Kendra finished her cold drink and said her goodbyes.

Dusty came in from the dining room where he'd been taking out a drawer he intended to fix for his mom. He stood in the kitchen, looking at the glass Kendra had used. *'I came here. I saw him. I fell in love with him all over again, even though I knew it was impossible for us to be together. I broke my own heart this time. Not Dusty. Not Erica or my mother. Me.'*

She blamed herself for this most recent disastrous outcome.

He set the drawer on the island.

His mother returned and stopped in her tracks. "I didn't know you were here."

"You must've been in the laundry room when I came in. I parked out back and used the side door."

"You heard that?"

"I heard."

"She loves you."

"I wish that fixed something, but it only makes it worse."

"I can't believe that."

"I'm taking this drawer with me. I forgot it the other day. All of your tablecloths are stacked on the table."

"Thank you." She picked up two glasses and carried them to the dishwasher. "I believe what I said to her, Dusty. Love finds a way."

"And I believe what she said. Not this time it doesn't."

He'd said all there was to say. He wasn't going to ask again for her forgiveness. It was tough not to live with a measure of hope, so he'd clung to mere shreds all this time. Maybe by Christmas seeing her wouldn't hurt as much.

❀

Kendra called the realtor who leased the house for her, letting her know when she'd be leaving and blocking out the weeks that she'd be returning over the Christmas holiday. She hadn't allowed herself to wonder how Dusty's legal counsel had gone. She had to distance herself somehow.

Kendra spent the morning working on choreography for the three songs she'd been sent by email. She decided to spend some time on the lake that afternoon, enjoying the sunshine while she could, so she put on sunscreen and her hat and took the boat out. An hour or so later, her phone rang and Joe's number showed up. "Hello?"

"Kendra, Joe here. Something has happened. Chloe wants you to come to the hospital."

"Chloe? Is she all right?"

"She took a fall is all. She was in Olde Town with friends.

The doctor thinks it's her ankle. She's in a lot of pain, and she wants you."

"Okay. On my way. I'm on the lake, so give me time to dock and drive there."

"You have time. We're in the ER, and nothing's happening very fast."

CHAPTER 12

*I*t took her nearly thirty minutes to store the boat, dress and drive into Spencer. The hospital took up most of a block with two connected buildings and parking lots. She parked in the ER lot and made her way inside. The admitting nurse buzzed her through a doorway and met her in the hall to show her to Chloe's room.

Joe stood dressed in his uniform, with a stricken expression wrinkling his forehead. "Thanks for coming. She's pretty distraught."

Chloe wore a pink t-shirt with glittery butterflies across the front, and shorts. Her leg was resting on two pillows and an ice pack had been wrapped around her ankle and foot. The whites of her eyes were as pink as her shirt, the lids puffy and her nose red. She had a bump on her forehead that was a raw scrape. She burst into tears. "Why did this have to happen to me now? I have to be able to audition for the academy."

Kendra leaned over and gave her a hug. She smoothed her hair away from her perspiring forehead. "Let's not get worried until we know more. Did you fall or twist your ankle?"

"Not really. It kinda just gave out on me when I was walking up some narrow stairs. I just fell."

"Your foot gave out on you?"

She nodded.

"Her whole foot looks swollen to me," Joe told her.

"Does it hurt?" Kendra asked.

"Oh yes, it hurts."

"Has it hurt before this?"

Chloe glanced sheepishly at her father and then back. "Yes. For a while."

"How long?"

"A couple of weeks."

Kendra glanced at Joe. "What tests have they done?"

"They did an X-ray just a little while ago. We're waiting on the doctor."

"What if I can't do the audition?" Chloe's lower lip trembled. This was obviously the worst thing she could imagine happening, and that was understandable.

"First, we don't know whether or not this would prevent you from auditioning. And second, if it should, you could wait another season, or we could take care of your tuition without the scholarship."

The teen appeared slightly comforted. At that age, a month felt like an eternity to wait for something this important.

"Is your head all right?"

"It looks awful, doesn't it?"

Kendra caught the girl's hand before she could touch the abrasion.

"Her pupils were fine," Joe explained. "Mom taught us bumps that show are good, because they're on the outside, not the inside."

Kendra smiled. She glanced aside. "I'm surprised I'm the only one here."

"Brooke has been in and out. She's taking care of other patients. Mom has to pick up Ian from daycare, and I didn't want to call others at work."

"I just wanted Dad to call you," Chloe said with a feeble smile.

Kendra pulled over a chair and sat beside her.

Within minutes the doctor arrived. "The X-ray doesn't show any broken bones, young lady. I think what you have is a sprained ankle."

Kendra caught his attention. "Doctor, may I ask a couple of questions?"

The slightly built balding man glanced at Joe and back at her. "Are you Mrs. Cavanaugh?"

"No, I'm Chloe's dance teacher and coach."

He looked at Kendra skeptically, but then must have recognized her. "You're the dancer who performed for the president, aren't you?"

"Yes, my academy performed in Washington," she answered, thinking she'd just garnered a little traction. "She has an important audition coming up, and we need to know exactly how bad this is. I'm familiar with dance-related injuries, and I was wondering if most of the swelling is on the back part of Chloe's heel?"

He looked at his patient, removed the ice packs and carefully examined Chloe's foot.

Kendra had stepped closer. "I don't see any bruising."

"It does appear the swelling is behind her ankle."

"I'd like to see her have an MRI and an ultrasound before treatment is decided," she suggested. "Chloe says she's had pain for a couple of weeks. I've had Achilles tendonitis misdiagnosed myself, so I'd be more comfortable with tests that can show tendons."

He stared at her for an uncomfortable moment but did a more thorough examination of the heel area. I can tell the Achilles isn't ruptured. I will however order the ultrasound. Meanwhile, I'll call our sports medicine ortho MD and consult with him."

He rewrapped Chloe's foot. He looked at her. "Have you been participating in strenuous activity?"

She nodded. "Is this worse than a sprained ankle?"

He patted her other foot. "No, but we want to treat it correctly for the most advantageous outcome." He turned to Joe. "I'll be back shortly."

"Thanks," Joe replied. After the doctor had left the room, he pulled a face at Kendra. "What was *that*?"

"Like I said, I've had this type of injury, as have a lot of dancers."

"I'm glad I called you."

"I told you to call her," Chloe interjected.

He nodded. "So, you did."

"If it's what you said, how long will it take to heal?" Chloe asked.

"Probably a few weeks, graduating to physical therapy."

Brooke came into the room in her blue scrubs. "Hi, Kendra." She stood beside her niece. "How's everything going? I saw orders for more tests."

"Kendra thinks it's a tendon something."

"Possibly," Kendra clarified. "It sounds like Achilles tendinitis, which dancers are prone to. I've had it."

"Not my field," Brooke said. "But if it is what you suspect, you'll save her the wrong treatment."

"A safer, quicker healing anyway."

"I wish I could just sleep," Chloe said. "It's really hurting, and I'm so tired."

"You probably exhausted yourself crying," Joe said. He

rubbed her other leg through the sheet. "It's going to be okay, baby girl. Brooke, is there something ordered?"

His sister rested her hand on Chloe's forearm. "Did they give you anything for pain yet? No? I'll go look on your chart and see what the holdup is. You should have meds before they move you around. They'll send a tech in here for the ultrasound. I'll be right back."

Thankfully, Chloe was given medication for the pain and relaxed, because it was another forty-five minutes before the tests were completed and thirty more minutes before the doctor came in to tell them he'd conferred with his colleague and they agreed it was indeed Chloe's tendon and heel causing the problem. The tendon was not torn, thankfully. The pain and swelling probably made her lose her balance and fall.

"We're going to wrap it, and then send you home in a cam boot with meds and crutches. You're to stay off your feet for several days, except to use the bathroom. We'll schedule an appointment with our sports medicine orthopedist as soon as possible and call you with that appointment. Meanwhile keep ice on that."

"I have a cold therapy unit she can use," Kendra offered.

"Better yet."

Joe's flat expression showed his dismay. While Brooke helped Chloe hop to the bathroom, he said, "I have vacation days, but I'll have to call around and see who can take my shifts."

Kendra didn't even think about it. "I can stay with her. It's not a problem. My class is finished, and I have the time."

"You can't do it alone."

Brooke had stepped out of the bathroom. "If we take her to Mom's, we can all take turns. Mom and Kendra and me. You can come after work," she said to Joe.

"Yes," Kendra agreed. "I can stay there with her. There's room for me, right?"

Brooke nodded affirmatively. "There's all kinds of room. Mom raised six kids in that house."

Joe picked up the bag with Chloe's shoes. "If you're sure you want to. You would be a big help."

A nurse brought a wheelchair, and Brooke helped the teen into it.

"Chloe, I'm going to go grab a few things from my house and then I'm coming to your grandma's to stay with you, all right?"

Chloe raised tired eyes to her dad. "Is it okay?"

"It's whatever you want, baby. Kendra thought it would be good if she and Brooke and Grandma take care of you while I'm at work. I'll come straight there after my shift. Kendra will probably be the one taking you to your appointments."

She nodded. "I like that idea."

Kendra headed toward the door. "The cold therapy unit takes a lot of ice, so I'll grab several bags on my way. We just fill the cooler and it runs cold water through a hose to a pad that can wrap around her foot."

"Thanks, Kendra. Having you here was really important to Chloe and she got better treatment because you knew what to look for." Joe gave her a hug as they parted ways in the parking lot, and Brooke pushed the wheelchair toward Joe's truck.

She hadn't thought twice about joining them at the hospital. Chloe was her star student, part of a family Kendra adored, and even if she hadn't been—she knew how terrifying an injury like that was. The pain brought every doubt and fear into focus. What if this needs surgery? What if I can't dance for a long time? What If I can never dance again? What if I lose my place in the company or the class or miss an audition? She knew too well how this kind of incident

struck dread into a dancer, young or not-so-young. She was
thankful her class had ended, and she had a few weeks left
before she had to go back to Denver. Feeling useful raised
her spirits.

❧

When Kendra arrived at Liz's, Chloe had already been settled
in a room on the main level. "This way when she's able to get
around, she won't have to take stairs," Liz said as she led
Kendra along the hallway. The large bright room had half-
shutters on four large windows, with light pouring in above
them. There were two double beds and a flat-screen television on the wall.

"You can stay in here, too," Chloe told her. "If you want."

"Sure. It's like college, only with a lot nicer room." She
stacked the couple of bags she'd brought and went back to
the car for the cold therapy machine. She added ice and
water in the kitchen, then carried it back to the bedroom
and plugged it in. She showed Liz and Joe how easy it was to
fill the cooler, plug in and turn on. "Then you wrap this
around the back of her ankle and foot and it stays cold for
hours."

"You must have had a lot of injuries to buy your own
gizmo like this," Joe said.

"I've had my share."

She suspected what he was thinking. "There are risks
involved with plenty of jobs," she said. "Sports injuries.
Driving injuries. Look at Brooke. Look at you."

"I know," he said. He looked over at his daughter, snug-
gled with a fuzzy blanket and her foot propped on pillows. "I
get it. You're right."

"When I was young…heck, when I wasn't young…I would
have given anything to have the support of a parent like you."

He nodded. "I want her to be happy. She's still my baby girl."

Kendra got a lump in her throat. She stepped forward and gave him a hug. "You're a great dad."

"Thanks."

It only took a few days for all of Chloe's friends and every last member of the Cavanaugh family to stop by for a visit. Colette brought Kyle and Avery, and the cousins hooked up a video game and hung out while Colette and Kendra cut and roasted all the butternut squash Colette had bought at a farmer's market. The prep had been Liz's idea on her way out to get groceries.

"She said we just cube it and stick it in the oven on these flat pans."

"With salt and onion and rosemary," Kendra remembered.

"That's in her garden. I'll grab it."

When it was finished, the roasted squash smelled incredibly good. They let it cool and then ran it through the blender in batches. Colette stirred the soup in a huge pan on the stove. "When she gets back with the cream, we'll add that."

"I've never done this before," Kendra said with a shrug.

"Neither have I." She turned the spoon over to Kendra. "I'm texting Tyler and telling him to come here for supper."

Of course, Crosby was there to eat as well. He'd showered upstairs and showed up with damp hair. The teens had set up trays and ate in the bedroom with Chloe, while the adults sat around the kitchen island.

"I don't know what you're doing these days, Crosby," she said to him. "You're outside all the time, that's obvious."

"I've worked lawn and landscaping for over six years. Got a business degree and I'm taking some basic engineering. I want to start my own business within the next couple of years. Startup is expensive, what with a building, trucks, equipment, insurance."

"Sounds like you know exactly what you need to do to make it happen. What about winter? Colorado winters are harsh."

"Which makes them lucrative too. All that snow needs to be moved out of parking lots and off private roads. Plows are an investment."

Impressed, she raised an eyebrow. "I always knew you were a smart kid."

"Tell that to my sisters who think I'm a slacker."

"No, they think you're a playboy."

"Where's the harm? I have my whole life to settle down."

"I don't have an opinion."

"Thank you."

After supper, everyone left, including Crosby. She and Chloe watched a movie until they both fell asleep.

❧

The next afternoon Liz left to pick up Ian after daycare. She fed and entertained him until Dusty arrived. She and Kendra had made pulled pork and slaw, so he stayed and had supper with his mom and Joe while Kendra ate with Chloe.

She left the bedroom and did dishes while Dusty and Ian hung out with Chloe. From the shouts coming from the hallway, it sounded as though they'd gotten involved in a video game.

"How are you doing?" Joe asked. Still in his uniform, he sat sipping a cup of coffee. "I know you're fine with Chloe and Mom, but I mean when Dusty shows up...are you handling that all right?"

She scrubbed the stainless-steel pressure cooker liner. "We're avoiding each other. It's working."

"How will you handle it when you go back to Denver?"

"Like I always have. The situation is not fixable. There's no solution. So, the only answer is to move on."

"Or you could forgive people."

Heat rose in Kendra's torso and crept up her neck. She rinsed the liner and set it on a drying mat. "You don't get it."

"I'm pretty sure I do. I know who your mother and sister are. I'll bet neither of them have asked for forgiveness. They probably don't even think they've done anything wrong. Neither of them deserves forgiveness."

"You've got that right."

"Well then start with Dusty. I know he's apologized. He's lived with the same consequences you have, and he took responsibility."

"I know that."

"Then forgive him for your own peace of mind. Forgive him before the anger and hurt eat you up inside. Do it for yourself, not for him."

She dried her hands and refused to look at him. "Are you the expert on forgiveness?"

"No. I'm the expert on holding in the anger until it ate me up inside."

She studied him with a new perception. Joe Cavanaugh was a big brawny lawman with a badge, but he spoke like a kindhearted man who cared. Well, he was a Cavanaugh. They came by this lovey-touchy-feely stuff naturally.

"Chloe's mom didn't deserve my forgiveness for running off and leaving her own kid. For leaving me with a baby to take care of. For leaving me to explain to my little girl that her mama wasn't coming back and to try to be everything she needed when I was broken myself. I had to forgive her for my well-being. So that I could pick myself up and heal. And that didn't start until I said the words.

"I get it. I know you don't want to forgive. But the anger

is going to chew you up until you do. You don't have to be friends with any of them. But you do need to let go of the anger." He got up, brought his mug to the dishwasher and placed it inside. "That's all I'm ever going to say to you about that."

He walked down the hallway toward the bedroom.

She carried the pressure cooker into the pantry, closed the door and stood there trembling. He was right. She was a terrible person, and he was right. She had never wanted to forgive them. Any of them.

She had some heart-searching to do. She'd had the strength to accomplish every difficult thing she'd ever set her mind to. Now she recognized the responsibility to take care of her own healing.

The last couple of days had shown her how this family showed up when one person needed help or attention. She'd witnessed what it was like to have others who supported and cared for each other. They'd been here for her all along too, she recognized that.

She'd seen the love of family she'd never known, except by the examples of these people, and she was thankful Chloe had that. Kendra was also thankful Ian had the very same family. Whatever happened in his life, he would always have this family.

Kendra stepped out of the pantry before someone discovered her. She felt foolish but relieved no one had seen her.

"We're going home now," Ian called, running across the kitchen.

She knelt and gave him a hug. "You have a great night."

"Can we go fishin' again with your boat?"

"I'm going to be here at your grandma's for a couple of weeks, but if your dad wants to, you guys can take it out any time you like."

"He's not going to let that one go," Dusty said apologetically, joining them. "He's focused on fishing this summer."

"That's okay. I love fishing, too, so I get it."

"I know Joe appreciates your help with Chloe. We've all seen how she idolizes you. You've probably relieved her fears by being here and by giving her someone to talk to."

"I'm happy to be here."

Their eyes met, and the familiar pull that was always under the surface came awake. She wanted to reach over and touch him, place her fingertips on the coarse texture of his cheek. She yearned to lean close and catch his scent. Oddly enough Jonas's words echoed in her memory. *'She was the one and only. That's a rare thing.'*

Dusty was undeniably her one and only. Her love for him had never grown cold. She acknowledged that as a fact.

And he said he'd never stopped loving her.

The night they'd spent together was fresh in her mind and on her heart.

Ian tugged on his hand. "Let's go, Dad."

She watched them leave, undeniably linked to them for all time, no matter where she was or how far she ran. She could never have family like theirs. Perpetually the outsider, she resigned herself to her independent life. She poured glasses of iced tea for herself and Chloe and headed for her room.

●

The following day she and Liz took Chloe to her appointment with the sports medicine ortho doc, and they got the expected diagnosis. The treatment was going well, so he told them to carry on as they were, but for Chloe to start letting the boot bear her weight.

Kendra drove through the Dairy Queen line and got them cones, then headed to a spot near the bridge on Chickering

Road and parked to look at the river. "I thought it would be nice to spend some time away from the house."

Chloe licked her ice cream. "It is. Thank you."

"The firemen are having their barbeque at Brook Park Friday night," Liz said. "We might as well get you out of the house for that. What do you think?"

Chloe grinned. "I could tell my friends I'll be there, and they'll come hang out. What about you, Kendra? Will you go?"

"And miss ribs served by hunky firemen? What do you think?"

They laughed.

"I ordered some books for you," Liz told her granddaughter. "Kendra, do you mind stopping by the bookstore?"

Kendra parked in front of the Rocky Mountain Bookstore. Liz ran in and returned with a small bag. "Kate had them all ready."

Chloe was tired after her outing, so Kendra got her settled, gave her the anti-inflammatory and pain pill, stacked her new books on the table beside the bed, and handed her the remotes.

"This is going to sound kind of silly," Chloe said.

"What?"

"Will you show me the videos again tonight?"

"Of course. That's not silly. You're encouraging yourself."

"And can we maybe watch a few of yours?"

"I have a few in the cloud we can grab."

"Girl's night?" Chloe asked with a smile.

"You've got it."

Kendra helped Liz with prep for the evening meal. Dusty called Liz to say he'd be getting Ian from daycare and going home, so not to set places for them. Kendra was more disappointed than she probably should have been. She couldn't imagine Chloe's frustration, because she'd begun to feel the restriction of these days as well. She would have appreciated a few hours on the lake, and she needed her morning routine to stay limber. She called Tina, who now ran the dance studio, about reserving time, and the woman offered her use of the facility any time she wanted. Using the studio in Spencer saved her the drive time of going home, so her new routine involved an early trip into town.

The interior had recently been painted, and there were a few new touches here and there, but the building was pretty much as it had been all the years Kendra had danced here with Aunt Sophie. She thought of all the little girls who'd been through the studio, from the toddlers in their frilly tutus to the girls and even a few boys who showed up hopeful and worked their young hearts out.

Framed photos of actual students in various poses added a personal and inspirational touch to the dressing rooms. She looked in each dressing room to see them all and found herself at about age fifteen. She touched the glass, barely remembering that girl.

Kendra went through her new choreography, taking notes, repeating sets, until the timer on her phone alerted her. She took a long drink of water and went into the dressing room that held her photo. That girl had been brave. She'd known what she wanted. She hadn't let her lack of means or the neglect stand in her way. Her situation had made her stronger. It had given her Sophie…and dance. She tried to see what Dusty had seen in her all those years ago. Something vulnerable maybe, yet a person with inner strength.

She'd always hated vulnerability. She'd worked her whole life to overcome weakness. These feelings she still dealt with every day, they weren't about vulnerability or strength. She was strong. These feelings were of deep hurt, abandonment, resentment and anger. It was exactly as Joe had said. Anger chewed up a person inside. She couldn't run from herself forever.

He'd made the solution sound so easy, but she'd fought it all along, quick to say she didn't want to forgive anyone.

Kendra dressed and put her dance clothes in her bag. She got her keys and went out to her car.

You've got this. What's the worst that can happen?

She got out her phone and scrolled for the number she wanted.

Two rings.

"Dusty here."

She didn't say anything. Hearing his voice closed up her throat. Made her heart beat erratically.

"Kendra?"

"Yeah. It's me." She put on her sunglasses and started the car. "I was wondering if we could talk."

"Now?"

"No. In person."

"Yes. Of course. Do you have a plan in mind?"

She hadn't thought this out. She was responsible for Chloe. "Maybe tonight while Joe is at the house with Chloe, your mom could watch Ian and we could go somewhere for a little while."

"Okay. I'll just check with Mom. I'm sure it will be fine."

"Thanks. I'll talk to you later."

"Okay." He hung up.

Maybe that strength she was so proud of was for this.

CHAPTER 13

*L*iz waved them off, and Dusty led Kendra out into the semi-darkness. Days were getting shorter. "Want me to drive?"

"Sure."

He opened the passenger door and she pulled herself up to the seat. He went around to the other side to get in. Starting the truck, he headed south. "Do you want food? Drinks?" He glanced over. "Beers at the lake?"

"I guess most of our serious talking has been at the lake, right?"

"There's spray repellant in the glove box."

"Then we're good."

After picking up a cold six pack at the carry-out, he drove around the north side of the lake. She'd been quiet during the drive, and he was trying to follow her lead. "I have some packing blankets behind the seat."

He proceeded to grab a couple and they made their way to a flat place on the bank, where he fashioned a cushioned place to sit and opened two bottles. "I was surprised to get your call. Honestly, I was surprised you're talking to me at all."

"Yeah, well that's what this is about."

He'd been waiting all day to know what she was going to say. The other evening in his mom's kitchen, something had passed between them, something that felt like the awareness that had always been electric between them.

"I can't live with the bitterness and anger anymore," she said.

She'd already made her plan to leave before Chloe's injury, so what was there to add to that?

"A couple of people have made me look at myself. At what unforgiveness is doing to me. It's not healthy."

He was glad she had people to talk to, but her vocalizing this with anyone still surprised him. She shut down whenever he tried to talk to her about this stuff.

"Joe said some things to me."

"If he was out of line—"

"He wasn't. He was spot on." She seemed to study the sky overhead. "You told me more than once that you were sorry. There's nothing more you could have done. You did it all exactly the way you should have. You apologized and you made it as right as you could. My hurt and anger has taken over since the start. I know you're a good dad, and I believe you always have Ian's best interests at heart. But I got angry at Erica trying to worm her way into your life—into our lives —all over again, and I barged in and made it ugly that day at Lacey's."

"I don't blame you for that. I wasn't mad at you. I wanted to throw her out too."

"But you have self-control. I don't know how, or where it comes from, but you do."

He shook his head. "I'm not letting you take the blame for any of this."

"No." She reached over and took hold of his wrist. "That's not what this is about."

He turned his hand over until he grasped hers. "What's it about then?"

There was still enough light as the sun lowered behind the mountains to see the raw emotion on her face. She turned to face him. "Look at me when I say this."

"I'm looking."

Her fingers trembled within his hold. She took a breath. "I forgive you."

Either the frogs and the crickets had all been silenced or his hearing had been compromised, because he couldn't hear anything save the echo of her words for a full minute. Eventually the nature sounds returned.

"I forgive you," she said again. "I didn't believe I was punishing you, but maybe I was trying to. I was definitely punishing myself, making it worse by hanging onto the anger all this time. I'm not angry with you. I don't know if I ever truly was. I was hurt, and I felt betrayed and insignificant."

Dusty's throat was so full of raw emotion, he barely managed to speak around it. "You were entitled to your feelings. We all were. I felt stupid. And embarrassed. And I didn't feel worthy of you. I wanted to earn your trust again, but I didn't know how."

"And I didn't let you." She released his hand and stood up, dropping her head back to look at the sky. "I can't tell you how good it feels to have said that."

"And maybe now you'll feel it too."

"Saying it made me feel it," she told him.

He reached for her hand and pulled her down to sit on his lap, with her bottom between his thighs. She wrapped her arm around his neck, and he pushed back the thick length of her hair and pressed his lips to her neck and jaw. Her hair was silky and her skin incredibly soft. He didn't even mind that she smelled vaguely of mosquito repellant. "Can we capture it again, what we had before? Can we find a way to just love each other?"

His eyes stung and he buried his face in her hair.

She wrapped her hand around his upper arm. "I don't know, Dusty. I wish we could."

"Say you want to try."

"I hope we can."

"There's never been anyone else for me," he told her with complete sincerity. "There never will be."

She raised her hand to cup his jaw and kissed him, a kiss like he remembered. A kiss that he craved and longed for with each day that passed. He had missed her more than he'd ever thought possible. Her presence, her love was the one last thing that would make his life complete. "Maybe if we start all over again…."

"Maybe." Her reply was a hoarse whisper.

He tumbled them back to lie on the padding. She kissed him until he knew she felt the same, but she was still afraid. She couldn't make the promises he wanted. He held her and they turned to gaze up at the stars in the night sky.

"It's not like this in the city," she said.

"It's always like this here, unless it's cloudy."

"I know."

"You have commitments in the city."

"I have a contract with a producer."

"So, you could work from anywhere."

"Theoretically. As long as I show up on the contracted dates."

He wasn't going to ask her more. He now suspected her Denver home was merely her hideaway from Spencer. Dusty felt more hope tonight than he'd had in a long time.

He wasn't going to push her. Or rush her. Or even suggest

anything. But he was going to show her exactly how good it could be between them.

❖

Dusty brought Ian for supper the next couple of evenings, and Kendra enjoyed their presence immeasurably. It became apparent to the others that something had happened between them to correct the stand-off. A couple of the family members were brave enough to comment. Dusty told Kendra his mom had asked him because she noticed they were 'quite cozy', in her words. Kendra told Joe she had taken the first step of forgiveness toward Dusty, and now every day was a little easier.

"That's a big step," he told her. They sat on the back patio, drinking coffee after dark while the others were inside.

"But, I know," she said. "Only the first step."

He nodded. "He asked for your forgiveness, and he deserved it. The others haven't asked, and they don't deserve it."

"So how do you do that?" she asked, really wanting to know. If she felt this much better already, she couldn't imagine how much she could improve.

"This wisdom isn't mine," he told her. "I saw someone for a while."

"A therapist?"

"Yeah. He told me to write down that I had forgiven my wife. So that's what I did. I wrote it on my calendar."

"Okay."

"After that, whenever those old feelings crept up on me, I'd pull out that calendar, flip to the page and say to myself, 'Nope. It's right there. I forgave her. That's over.'"

"And it worked."

He nodded. "Not that very minute, but over a few weeks,

yes, it did. But I even got out the calendar a year later and looked at it to remind myself."

She took a sip of her coffee. It had cooled off, and she grimaced.

"You know our folks raised us in church," he added. "I'd heard teachings about forgiveness all my life. When we were kids my mom told us to apologize and forgive each other and we did. But I thought that was only for people I loved and who loved me. People who regretted their mistakes. I had never taken it to heart as being a requirement toward a person who had truly hurt me and didn't have any regrets about their actions. I didn't think it applied to a person who didn't deserve it. My wife didn't deserve my forgiveness."

"Did you ever hear from her again?"

"Not personally, but I heard through other sources that she'd contacted old friends and was living in Alaska. I had to hire a detective to find her to serve her with divorce and custody papers."

Kendra didn't say 'at least she's gone' because she didn't want to minimize what Joe had gone through. She wished her sister had run off to Alaska. She wouldn't hire a detective.

"I never knew who my father was," she told him. "I asked a couple of times and Lacey brushed off my questions. I suspect she didn't know or remember."

"Ever think about trying one of those ancestry sites that finds your relatives?"

"Oh, heck no. I have a feeling I'd be really, really sorry. I have enough issues with the family I do know about."

"Sometimes I think about that. Chloe knows what happened. Someday, though, she might try to find her."

"Which will be her right."

"Absolutely. I'll help her if that time ever comes."

"Joe?"

"Hmm?"

"Will you be my dad?"

She joined his burst of laughter.

❖

She thought about everything Joe had shared. He'd been very forthcoming with her about what he'd gone through. She didn't know if even fifteen years put enough time between a person and their heartbreak, but he seemed to have worked through it enough to offer his experience. She used her phone app to schedule her life, but she pulled it up and looked at it, remembering how Joe had told her what he'd written on his calendar.

"Kate Michaels sells calendars at her store, doesn't she?" she mused aloud the following day in the kitchen.

Liz looked up from putting a glass inn the dishwasher. "Yes, I've seen a rack of calendars. Do you need one?"

"I was thinking about getting one."

"Oh, don't buy one this late in the year. Let me find you one." She went into the pantry, pulled down a basket and rifled through an organized bundle. "I get so many from the Disabled Veterans and the American Heart Association, March of Dimes and all the lists I'm on. I save them for the kids to cut out pictures." She carried a stack to Kendra. "Take whatever you like."

Kendra chose one with scenic photographs and thanked her. Later, after Chloe had fallen asleep with the television on and Kendra lay comfortably on the other bed, she opened the calendar to the current month and day. She stared at it until her eyes blurred.

A clean slate. Nothing had been written or scheduled all year. Chloe's felt tip pens were lying on the night table atop a 'million cats' adult coloring book. Kendra picked up a teal one, removed the cap and let the pen hover over the page.

She swallowed hard. Looked over at her sleeping young friend. The girl's mother had deserted her as an infant. Left her husband—*Joe*—with a new baby to take care of. She'd known Joe for years, knew him better after this week. What kind of person walked out on a man like that? But he'd forgiven her. Written it down as his first step to healing.

Her hesitation stabbed her with self-disgust. She jabbed the lid back on the pen and returned it. After dropping the calendar on the floor beside the bed, she turned out the light.

Tomorrow was another day.

❦

Chloe was up to attending the fireman's barbeque on Friday evening, so Kendra rode with Liz, Joe and Chloe in Joe's Tahoe. They brought the wheelchair so Chloe wouldn't have to maneuver over the uneven ground in the awkward black boot. Kendra knew a lot more people this time than she had the last, and she was immediately greeted by welcoming locals.

Glen Randall, carrying a sleeping infant, spotted her and brought his wife over to meet her. "Kendra! This is my wife, Ashley—and our new daughter, Joy."

Ashley was lovely, with dark hair and eyes. She smiled.

"Hi, Ashley." The baby had a tuft of dark hair, full smooth cheeks and a little rosebud pink mouth. Her mom had a lightweight cotton wrap under her, but her tiny legs and feet were bare in the summer evening for now. "She's just precious," Kendra breathed with awe. "So perfect and beautiful."

The new parents smiled at each other.

"Sorry about ditching your call the day you arrived," Glen

told her. "Dusty said he handled your situation, and all was well."

"Well, I think you had more important things to tend to that day." She smiled at their little family. "I'm really happy for you." She turned to Glen. "I left you a message the other day. I'm not leaving as soon as I'd intended. I'm staying to help out with Chloe, Dusty's niece and my student. She had an injury, but she's on the mend."

"I got your message. No worries. You just call me when you're leaving, and I'll come check out the house for the next renters."

"Thanks, Glen."

Glen was someone she depended on to take care of her house. The couple walked away, and she made a mental note to send a gift. Something pretty for a dark-haired baby girl.

Loydell was there and introduced her to a short heavyset man, probably fiftyish. Did Loydell have a man friend? "Kendra, hon, this is Reuben Trumbull. You might recognize him as—"

"The gentleman who delivers my mail," Kendra finished. She'd never seen him out of his truck or without his cap. Her mailbox was big enough to hold most packages, but she'd walked out to give him little gifts now and then.

"And you're Kendra Price, the young lady who makes rhubarb tarts and the most amazing salsa I've ever had."

"Oh, well, thank you." She grinned, pleased he had appreciated her offerings and remembered her.

"Not only does Reuben deliver the mail with excellence, he plays a mean game of pool."

"I'll keep that in mind."

When she looked for Chloe, she found a group of the teen's friends surrounding her. Joe nodded at her from a distance. He was keeping an eye on his daughter. Kendra still hadn't taken his advice. But she didn't feel as bad as she had before, because at least now she wanted to, and that was progress.

She strolled through the groups of people until she found Piper with Brianna. They moved apart almost guiltily. "Hey, Kendra," Piper said.

"What's going on?" she asked. "You two look like the cat that swallowed the canary, as my Aunt Sophie would have said. Were you talking about me?"

"Not you, exactly. But something that will affect you."

"What is it?"

"There's someone I need you to meet," Brianna told her.

"Okay."

The dark-haired young woman took out her phone and texted someone. A ping indicated the response. She tilted her head. "Over here."

She led them a distance to the other side of the gazebo. There were a few band members setting up their equipment, but a slender man stood fifty feet away. They joined him. Up close, the tattoos on his knuckles were visible; he had a scrawny mustache and goatee, and a scar on the bridge of his nose.

"This is Shane. Shane this is Piper and Kendra. Kendra is the one who will be interested in what you have to say."

"It's kind of embarassin'." He gave an awkward shrug and glanced between the women.

"Don't be embarrassed around them. They won't judge you." Brianna gave him an encouraging nod.

"Me an' my friends, we hang out at the Trail's End. Play pool, throw back a few brewskys, you know."

"Sure," Piper said. "We like to chill on the weekends too."

"Well, I met this chick a while back. Not bad lookin', kinda clingy, but good for a few dances and a laugh, you know the type."

"We do," Piper answered.

Kendra was beginning to suspect where this was going.

"Some of us snuck a few beers out to the parking lot. Now I can handle my booze, and nothin' like that night ever happened to me before. I was havin' fun bullshittin' and next thing I remember was wakin' up in my truck at dawn the next day."

"Tell her the name of the person you'd been with that evening," Brianna urged.

"Erica Price. The other fellas knew who she was." He rubbed his neck and glanced around before going on. "I went to see a couple of 'em, and we got to thinkin' my blackin' out didn't make sense. My buddy told me to go get tested at the clinic, so I did."

Kendra's heart was beating a mile a minute. "What came of that?"

"I had liquid A in my bloodstream."

"What's that?" Kendra asked.

"Date rape drugs," Piper supplied.

"Hell, there's recipes for this shit on the Internet," Shane added. "Docs called the sheriff and a deputy came to take a statement. They asked me to press charges, but I told 'em I needed to think about it. It could be embarassin' for my folks."

Kendra couldn't catch her breath for a moment and clasped her hands to keep them from trembling. She breathed in an out to calm her quaking nerves. "I think this happened to someone else we know," she managed to say. And she hadn't given him the benefit of the doubt. "Thank you for telling us. Will you let Brianna know if you do press charges?"

"Sure will."

She stuck out her hand. "I can't thank you enough for telling me."

Shane titled his head in acknowledgement.

"I'm going to talk to Joe." She took off at a half run.

She found him with Aunt Cora and Kate Michaels, and greeted them, trying not to be rude, but to get him off to the side.

"What's up with you?" he asked.

"Have you had any reports of men who suspected they'd been drugged or have been tested for liquid A?"

"GHB?"

"I guess so. The person blacks out for hours and can't remember what happened."

"I'd have to go through reports to see, but I don't have any charges on record that I remember. Why are you asking?"

"Brianna just introduced me to a man who'd tested positive for the drug. And guess who he was with the night before?"

"I have no idea."

"Erica."

His expression changed the moment he realized what she was saying. "Is he pressing charges?"

"Not yet. But one of your officers made a report at the clinic and encouraged him to do so."

"Are you going to tell Dusty?" he asked.

"Yes. He has hated himself this whole time. For six years. I'm going to tell him."

"We don't have proof she did this to him."

"I don't need any more proof than this."

He nodded. "I'll search reports first thing in the morning."

She took off in search of Dusty.

❧

Dusty had parked his truck in the church lot across the street from the park. Music from the bandstand echoed across to where he and Kendra sat in the dark with the windows down. The local band was covering *If I Can't Have You* and doing a decent job. The past half hour had been a revelation of epic proportions, and he still couldn't quite wrap his mind around it.

"I'm sorry, Dusty."

"Why would you be sorry?"

"Because I was angry for so long. Angry with *you*."

"We don't know this is what happened for sure," he said.

"I think we do. Joe is going to find similar reports that will lead back to Erica. She's been getting away with this for a long time. You said you didn't remember anything that happened that night."

"I don't."

"Had anything like that happened before or has it happened since?"

"No, of course not."

"Because, for whatever reason, she chose you that night. I have always known she was mean. I've always known she hated me. But she outdid herself with this one. At the expense of people's lives."

He couldn't disagree with that. After all this time of berating himself for being in the wrong place at the wrong time and getting stupid drunk, and now learning that what happened probably hadn't been his fault after all was almost too good to be true.

He got out his phone and looked up the drugs. "This stuff could be disastrous and cause an overdose. Why would she do this?"

"She probably did it because she wanted to hurt me," Kendra said. "She used you to play out some stupid scheme that she thought would keep me from being happy. Which it did, so if that was the plan, she got what she wanted."

"Apparently female perps are way more common than

people think. This is perfect," he blurted and looked up from his phone.

"What?"

"Once that Shane person files charges, or some more guys come forward, I have the perfect information to take to a judge to keep her from seeing Ian. Even Lacey couldn't shrug this off. It's sick."

"It sounds like one of those *Dateline* stories, doesn't it? Truth that's stranger than fiction?"

He pounded his fist soundly on the steering wheel. "I wish it wasn't my truth."

Kendra took his hand and slid over beside him. She brought his fist up, straightened his fingers and rested them along her cheek. "She used you to hurt me. I'm so sorry, Dusty."

"It's not your fault. Don't apologize to me again. Please."

"We're going to get through this."

"That's the first time you've ever said that."

"It's the first time I've ever felt it could happen."

For the first time, he felt hope for them, as well. But there would certainly be publicity. "I don't want my son to be known for this. I don't want him to be ashamed, and you know he would be, even though it's not his fault—or mine."

"Your brother will help us. A judge will understand. They will keep Ian out of this."

"I won't go forward if they don't promise that. I can't."

"Of course. What she did to you can't be made public," she agreed, relieving part of his concern.

"I'll come home with you guys and tell my mom."

"She will be relieved too."

She gave him a kiss full of promise, not only of the possibility of their relationship, but of a future where this wasn't always their main concern, like a wall slamming up between them. He was so tired of it, but now it looked as though there was a way out of the impossible.

Shock showed on Liz's face when she got the information, but then she sat at the island, buried her face in her hands and her shoulders shook.

Dusty rubbed her back. "It's going to work out now, Ma. The truth is going to come out, but we'll protect Ian."

Kendra brought her some tissues, and she wiped her eyes. "I never thought less of you, Dusty. But now I feel guilty for even thinking you might have had some responsibility."

"I thought the same thing, so no one has to feel guilty." He rubbed her shoulder.

"All the years the two of you have missed out on," she said, looking up at Kendra through tears.

Kendra's eyes glistened too. "We can't focus on that," she said with a sniff. "We all did what we had to do or what we thought we needed to do, and we got through it to here and now. From this day on is what's going to count. Not the past...the future."

Dusty reached for her, and she moved against his side. He held the two women he loved with a new sense of assurance. "Will you two keep Ian here with you tomorrow? I want to go with Joe while he checks reports."

"As long as you promise to let us know when you find something," Kendra said.

"Can I have some popcorn?" Ian came from Chloe's room. "What are you guys doing?"

"Hugging. You ate a hot dog, chips, ice cream and watermelon. You don't need popcorn before you go to bed. You'll have crazy dreams."

"I want to dream I'm a pirate," he announced.

"That's not how dreams work," Dusty said and lifted him into his arms. "How big will you be when I can't pick you up and hug you anymore?"

"Maybe twelve. Or thirteen."

"Thank you for believing in me, son. What if you're a really big twelve-year-old?"

"I'll pick you up then."

Liz laughed and Dusty hugged his son. "Let's get you home to bed. You're coming back to hang with Grandma and Kendra in the morning."

"All right!"

After telling Chloe goodnight, they parted on that cheerful note. There was so much on his mind, he didn't know how he'd sleep, but tomorrow was a new day.

CHAPTER 14

*D*usty didn't call until afternoon. Kendra held her phone so Liz could hear too.

"Joe found a couple of reports, and I sat in his vehicle while he went to the guys' homes and questioned them. One is married and won't take this any further. The other is willing to file charges. And get this. Erica even came to them both afterward asking for money for an abortion. The married guy gave it to her. This other one didn't. He asked for proof of a pregnancy, but all she had was a couple photos on her phone."

"Is he filing the charges today?"

"Yes. He's coming to the station now."

"Then they'll pick her up?"

"Yes. She'll get a public defender."

"Joe will make sure the records are sealed for Ian's privacy, though?"

"Yes. He's working on this. It's a level two drug felony, so by law she is due a trial by jury. It would be in her favor and everyone else's to choose a bench trial, however, so her lawyer will encourage that choice."

"Before a judge only."

"Right."

"Will she be in jail today then?" Liz asked.

"I'm not sure," Dusty answered. "If she gets to see a judge immediately, he might set bail before the hearing."

"How can she pay bail?" Kendra asked.

"Her lawyer would get a bondsman to pay it."

"Unbelievable," Liz said.

"It's going to be okay," Dusty told them. "She's being exposed. That's what counts."

"You're right." Kendra thanked him and ended the conversation.

"This is going to make her furious," she told Liz. "Erica finds every means available to place the blame for her behavior on others. She will play her poor-me role to the max. No one has seen her angry."

Liz sat down, but she looked at Kendra. "Do you think Lacey should have a heads up about this?"

Kendra considered her suggestion before answering. "She would think warning Erica was protecting her, so no. I don't think that would be wise. It would cause more problems."

"You're right." She glanced around the kitchen. "What do you say we eat out this evening? I'll ask Chloe if she's up to it, and whoever is here at mealtime joins us."

"That's a great idea. Where do you want to go? We can guess at reservations."

"We could do Mexican or Chinese. At China Buffet we don't need reservations."

"Ian likes it?" Kendra asked.

"He loves it."

"Okay, let's do Chinese."

"No dinner prep. That gives us time to do something else."

"Go Fish?"

"No. It's nice out. We could do a little gardening. Let Chloe get some sun."

"Who wants to go outside and play?" Kendra called down the hallway.

✤

After church on Sunday, Joe brought the news that a judge had immediately set bail for Erica on Saturday evening, since Monday was Labor Day and she would have been left in the county jail until Tuesday.

"Her lawyer didn't ask for a preliminary hearing right away, so the court date is set for four weeks from now."

"Four weeks?" Dusty had asked. "Giving her attorney time to put a defense case together?"

"And giving the prosecuting attorney time to build our case," Joe added. "We have this. They took her phone right away and entered it into evidence. We have you and two others willing to press charges."

"I don't have drug testing evidence, though."

"Our star plaintiff does."

"Shane," Kendra said.

Joe nodded.

"Let's set all this aside and enjoy our holiday tomorrow," Liz suggested. "What shall we do? Cook out?"

"Why don't we cook out at my place?" Kendra suggested. "We can set up some tables and chairs, a canopy for shade. Anyone with experience can take the boat out. I don't have life jackets for the kids though."

"Tyler and Colette have plenty in all sizes," Dusty said. "They have tables and lawn chairs in their garage too." He got out his phone and texted his older brother who was spending the afternoon with Colette's folks.

"Well, that's all set," Liz said cheerfully. "Let's plan a menu in case I need to run for groceries."

Brooke entered in jeans and sandals. "What's all set?"

"The holiday at Kendra's lake house tomorrow."

"Nice." Brooke grinned. "Can I bring a date?"

Dusty and Joe pounced on that question.

"Who is he?"

"You're seeing someone?"

"Do we know him?"

Kendra laughed as their pink-faced sister fended off the attention.

Stephanie stepped in through the back door. "I could hear you outside. What's all this about?"

The good-natured inquisition started all over again. The Cavanaugh's laughter warmed Kendra's heart, reminding her that life went on around her. This experience with Dusty didn't have to be the thing that defined either of them or their relationship.

It couldn't be. She had to put it in its place and move on with her life.

Later that night, she and Dusty went for a ride in his truck, parked at the lake and allowed themselves to talk about what would happen after all this was behind them. They didn't say the word 'marriage', but Dusty asked her, "So you could conceivably do your choreography from here and travel for your contracted meetings and appearances?"

"Conceivably, yes."

"What about performing? Do you want to perform again?"

"I've worked myself away from that aspect, for a lot of reasons. The commitment, the competition, the travel. It's life on the road, living in hostels or hotels. Rehearsals at daybreak, injuries, hunger…." She studied his face. "I love dance. It *is* my passion, but that part of it stole so much of the joy. Plenty of others thrive in that atmosphere." She shook her head. "I didn't."

"So, before you came here this summer, you had already been moving away from performing?"

"I love to teach, and helping the students understand their maturing bodies is more important to me now. I had several good years, but my focus has changed."

"It's a loss to the world, I can say that for sure."

"There are a lot of dancers waiting to fill my place."

"I can't even explain how it made me feel to see you dance."

"I'll still dance for you."

He hugged her tightly. "Promise?"

"I'll dance with you, too."

Dusty reached for the touchscreen on the dash and brought up a playlist. "What's your choice?"

"You choose."

He touched a selection by Ed Sheeran, turned up the volume and got out. She met him in front of the truck under the summer night sky. A shiver of pleasure went up her spine as the song began and Dusty reached for her.

'I found a love...for me....'

She couldn't have spoken if her life depended on it. She could hardly breathe. She rested her head on Dusty's shoulder and the world disappeared. He was strong and solid and warm. She wanted to lose herself in him and stay right here forever.

She loved the words to this song, the rhythm and the perfection of music and lyrics. The vocalist sang of a slow kiss, and she closed her eyes. How fitting that Dusty had chosen this song.

'...dancing in the dark... with you between my arms....'

He moved her back a fraction so he could look at her. They could have been teenagers for the carefree pleasure they enjoyed in that moment, the rush of adrenaline and the heady anticipation of a future together.

It was too soon to say the words, but the promise was there all the same. Only a few more weeks, and they would be free of the past.

The last notes of the song floated across the lake, leaving behind the sound of the steady lapping of the water—a sound as constant as the emotion that pulsed between them.

"I love you, Dusty."

"I can see the future in your eyes," he whispered.

"Were you always this romantic?"

"Only from the moment I met you."

❦

The sun kissed the day with its appearance that morning, burning the fog off the lake and waking the wood ducks with their ducklings. Kendra had slept at the lake house the night before, so she went through her stretches and performed the routines a few times, taking notes. She had brought the calendar in her overnight bag, and she'd thought about it long into the night.

Nothing about her situation had actually changed. Except her heart. She needed to relieve herself of the rest of this burden, so she could truly move on. She went for a pen and returned to her bedroom to open the calendar to Labor Day. She clicked the pen tip out and drew a box around the date. Then deliberately and with her breath held, she printed the words in the little box.

I forgive my mother.
I forgive Erica.

She exhaled. She hadn't referred to Lacey as her mother in fifteen or more years. She studied the words on the calendar page. Looked up. The earth hadn't shaken. Sun still poured through the white wood blinds creating rows of light and dark across her bed and the dark wood floor. But she felt lighter as she tucked away the calendar.

She went straight to the small carved box on her bureau and opened the lid. From the velvet-lined interior, she found a serpentine sterling chain and dropped the pendant that had been on it back into the box. With her thumb and forefinger, she picked up her engagement ring and slid it on the chain. She checked the latch and pulled on it while it was closed a few times to make sure it was secure, and then fastened the clasp behind her neck and tucked the ring beneath her 'good things come to those who bait' t-shirt.

Tyler and Colette arrived first, their vehicle loaded with tables, chairs, and lifejackets. Tyler and the kids unloaded and carried tables around to the back while Kendra took Colette in to show her to the kitchen.

"I love this place," Colette said with an enthusiastic lift to her voice. "I mean *love it*. I always imagined your place would look like a cabin. All the cabins on the lodge side are elegant but constructed and decorated very rustic."

"My Aunt Sophie built this place in the sixties, and it was quite modern for its time. She liked simple, but she didn't like wood interiors. I updated it with a new fireplace and all the floors. New appliances of course, added on the back sunporch."

"It's gorgeous. So bright and the rooms are large. It's very homey. Your renters must love it."

"The same visitors come back often," Kendra agreed.

"I brought makings for a seven-layer salad. Can I get started?"

"Sure. I'll help you." She took the bundles of lettuce

Colette handed her and washed them. She glanced at the blond-haired woman a little sheepishly. "This is the first time I've had anyone over besides Dusty and Ian."

Colette stopped peeling hard-boiled eggs to give her a little smile. "I'm seeing your confidence grow to include more than dancing," she said. "You're beginning to accept that others see you as strong and capable and that plenty of people care about you. We've always seen you that way, but you never saw it in yourself. It was tough growing up here. Maybe you needed to get away to see who you are outside of Spencer, Colorado. Then once you knew your worth, you could come back and be that person you discovered."

"I like that thought," Kendra told her. "It makes my time away important."

"Of course, it was important. Look at who you've become."

"I'm thinking I can live here now. Work from Spencer."

"And be fulfilled?"

Kendra smiled. "Absolutely. Nothing will be decided until the hearing is behind us though. The future is still up in the air. Our main concern is to protect Ian."

"As it should be."

Noise came from the front of the house as more Cavanaughs arrived. Wearing white capris and a bright pink top, Liz carried in a pot of baked beans and set it on the stove. "Oh, my goodness, Kendra. Your house!"

"It would fit in a corner of yours, but I love it," she answered.

"I was here many years ago when your Aunt Sophie was alive. It looked nothing like this."

Brooke and Steph arrived together, so she gave them all a tour of the rest of the house and her studio upstairs.

"I can just see you dancing in here," Steph said with a sigh. "If I have a little girl, will you be her instructor?"

Kendra blinked. "Yes, I'd love to."

"Leave it to Steph to plan ahead," Brooke joked. "Do you have her name picked out?"

"I'm not telling you."

Once everyone had arrived and the meal was ready, Tyler said a blessing over their food, and they dug in. Kendra couldn't have been happier than to have these friends here, enjoying themselves.

Tyler helped Avery and Kyle set up their badminton net, and they formed teams, including Ian. It wasn't long until he wanted to take the boat out on the lake though, so Dusty took him, along with Tyler, Avery, Kyle and Chloe, out to enjoy time on the water.

Colette made sure all of the kids wore lifejackets.

Liz covered the food and Kendra brought out a chilled bottle of wine and glasses. Joe, Crosby and Brianna deferred to cold beers from the cooler.

"It's so beautiful here," Liz commented, turning her face up to the sun. "I was so happy to hear you'd been able to keep the place for yourself."

"It took some doing, but I couldn't let it go. There are a lot of good memories here."

They tried their hand at badminton for a while. Crosby hit the birdie so hard, he was always making them duck, and they laughed until Kendra got a stitch in her side. She and Liz left to sit out a match, while the girls tried to beat him at his hard-hitting style.

"We can't let the kids see us do this," Colette warned. "Someone will get clobbered with a racket."

"Look at all that rhubarb," Crosby said, coming back to the cooler. "No wonder you're a never-ending source of goodies.

Kendra laughed. "I know. I thin it out, too, but the soil is so dark and nutrient rich along here, it just grows and grows. If any of you want some of your own, I'll dig it out for you."

"I'll take some," Liz said. "I'll help you dig it."

Kendra got pails and a shovel from the shed. Joe took the shovel from her.

She heard the sound of Dusty and Tyler returning with the kids and went to meet them.

"There's other boats on the lake," Ian told her. "Fast ones too."

"Probably tourists," Dusty said. "There's a no wake zone for the fishermen."

"What's no wake?" the boy asked.

"We shouldn't make big waves," Kendra explained. "Plus going fast on this end of the lake isn't safe for anyone who doesn't know what they're doing."

"I pulled the boat onto the bank until the next excursion," Dusty told her.

She leaned into him, and his arms went around her.

"Nothing feels as good as this," he whispered to the top of her head.

"Nothing?"

"Don't be going there."

She leaned back and raised up for a kiss.

Dusty licked his lips. "Did you open the wine without me?"

"Come on. Joe's digging rhubarb for your mom."

"You should put up a stand on the highway."

"I've thought about leaving bags on people's porches, ringing the bell and just running."

Dusty got a soda from the cooler.

Colette was making a place on a blanket in the shade for Chloe. "What's for dessert?" Chloe asked. She glanced at Kendra. "Is it rhubarb pie?"

Kendra laughed. "No, you're spared today. It's strawberry shortcake."

The sound of a car door slamming got her attention. Kendra walked through the side yard toward the front of the house.

Spotting Erica walking toward the front door startled her. "What are you doing here?"

Erica changed direction. "Apparently not entertaining all of my rich friends who have fancy cars, like you are."

There *were* some pretty nice cars lined along her driveway and in front of her house.

"Pretty convenient that you're screwing the sheriff's brother, so you could sic him on me with these made-up charges to get me out of your hair."

"Everything okay, Kendra?" Colette asked, coming around the corner of the house.

"Take all the kids into the house and have them help you with the dessert," Kendra said so only Colette could hear her.

Immediately Colette turned and hurried away, passing Dusty and Liz, who were headed toward her. "What is it?" Liz asked.

Dusty spotted Erica.

"Well, if it isn't the poor victim?" Erica called, hurrying toward them. "Do you have them all believing your sad story now?"

"I can't talk to her," Dusty said. He turned and headed away.

"Get Joe," his mom said quickly.

Erica followed after him. "I'd like to talk to Joe too."

"You can't be here," Kendra said. "None of us have anything to talk about. It will be handled at the hearing."

Her sister marched to the backyard and looked around. She put her hands on her hips. "Well, isn't this fancy? Looks like a dinner party right out of the magazines with your tablecloths and dishes and wine glasses. And check it out! All of your Cavanaughs in one place to give you all the attention you missed out on in your real family. Isn't that sweet?" She turned toward Kendra. "I'm your *real* family, you know. Not these puffed up do-gooders who felt sorry for you. Poor pitiful Kendra. Look at the dump she lived in and the pathetic excuse for a mother she had. Look at her no-good sister. Let's all make daisy chains and sing *Kumbaya*. Let's send her to college and buy her a house."

Joe took several steps toward the sisters, his limp more pronounced than usual. The others kept their distance.

"No one sent me to college," Kendra pointed out. "I earned scholarships and worked every waking moment. No one paid for dance academy either. I bought this house with money I earned myself."

"Really? I see it a whole lot differently. Sucker Sophie gave you a leg up. She babied you and taught you to dance."

"You could have danced if you'd wanted to. No one stopped you."

"You were the shining star, Kendra. Not me. I was the clumsy gawky girl with the plain brown hair and a nasty streak."

"I certainly didn't feel pretty or special either."

"You must have been, because you found a new family who wanted you. You have all this, and I have nothing. You ruined me by finding those men to tell stories!" Her voice rose. "You have the law after me now, and I have no choices."

"You've had choices your whole life, Erica. As many as I had."

"Shal I point it all out again? I didn't have a Sophie. I didn't have a back-up family. I don't have a house." She looked at Joe. "Don't come any closer to me."

"I paid for my half of the house, remember?"

Erica clenched her fists. Rage distorted her features. "Oh, I remember. I got a check I could sleep with at night, right?"

"I don't care what you did with the money."

"I couldn't exactly buy a boat, could I? Since I don't have a boathouse or a lake."

She wanted to say she didn't own the lake or plenty of people docked boats at the marina, but Kendra was finished arguing with her. It was obvious Erica wasn't capable of listening or of even rational thinking at this point. She had heaped a mountain of perceived slights upon Kendra's head and had no intention of hearing reason.

"You never invited me over here."

Kendra tried not to let her chin drop after that statement. "After what you did, Erica? Really?"

"You didn't know what I did. I'm your *sister*. You never gave me the time of day. I should have known you were the one buying my half of the house."

"You wouldn't have let me have it, if you'd known."

"Because you had *everything*!"

"I think it's time for you to calm down and leave," Joe said.

"I don't give a damn what you think," she said, turning her anger on him. "Or any of you!" She glared wild-eyed at the others standing in surprise after having their pleasant day crashed. "In fact, I think I'll have a glass of wine. Maybe go for a boat ride." She skirted the table, picked up a half-full glass of wine as though she was going to take a drink, and then threw it toward Kendra. The glass landed harmlessly on the grass.

"Whoa," Dusty said, stepping forward as though to protect Kendra.

At that she swiped dishes off the table with a sweep of her arm. "You told everyone what I did!" She stood with her arms rigid, breathing hard.

Kendra had no words for her, but Erica wouldn't have listened anyway. Her behavior was becoming frightening, and Kendra was thankful Colette had the children inside.

Erica started around the table. Kendra awaited her next outburst. When her infuriated sister reached the other side, she didn't throw more food or drinks as anticipated, instead she took off at a run.

The gathering simply watched her for a few stunned moments with no one moving.

Kendra's gaze followed her sister as she ran toward the lake. "What the—?"

"Oh, no. The runabout." Dusty took off at a run.

Crosby and Joe followed.

"Can she operate a boat?" Tyler asked.

"I have no idea," Kendra answered with a shake of her head. She headed after the others.

Erica'd had too long of a lead and reached the shored ahead of them. Several false starts and the engine started. Kendra arrived at the bank with the others as her aluminum runabout headed out onto the open water of the lake with Erica at the rear steering. "She's going too fast," she said.

"Does she know what she's doing?" Joe asked.

"I don't know."

"There are submerged trees out there. She won't know where to avoid them." Dusty's voice showed his concern.

"We can't go after her unless I go find another boat," Joe said.

Dusty put his hands on his head and watched with obvious dread. "And she's going too fast for that to help."

Joe turned to stop his mother and Brianna from joining them at this vantage point. "You should go on back."

"Why?" Liz asked. "Is she in danger? Can we call someone?"

Joe got out his phone. "I'll call Recreation and Parks. They have patrol boats and they'll be on the lake today." He spoke to an officer and gave him the information.

"Can you still see her?" Crosby asked.

Joe barely shook his head. "No, she's out of sight toward the dam."

"There are shallows that direction." Panic stole Kendra's breath. She put her hands to her lower face, still straining to see.

"I think I hear the engine," Dusty said. "There she is, heading back from that inlet that goes under the dam bridge."

"That's not good," Kendra said. "This end isn't cleared like the north and west sides. What was she thinking?"

Dusty turned and wrapped his arms around her. She trembled in his embrace. He cupped her head and drew her face against his shirtfront.

An explosion came then, echoing across the lake.

Kendra jerked from his hold. Smoke billowed up into the sky and flames spilled across the top of the water.

They stood in silent horror, watching helplessly as flames licked at remnants of the boat and the gas burned on the surface of the water.

"She must've hit something with the motor and knocked it into the gas tank," Joe said. As soon as that gas hits the battery...."

In all the years Dusty had known Kendra, he'd never seen her cry. Staring at the wreckage, she burst into tears. "We should have stopped her!"

Liz went to her and wrapped an arm around her. "Honey, we had no idea she was going to take the boat."

"I know. I know," she sobbed. She looked up. "She could still be alive."

"We'll wait for the patrol to get back to me," Joe said.

Dusty stood in front of her. "You know how unlikely that is, don't you?"

She straightened and nodded. The aluminum runabout steered from the rear where the prop, gas tank and battery were. Anyone sitting there when the boat exploded would be in the heart of the blast. "I'll have to tell Lacey."

Joe answered calmly, "Let's give the patrol time to do their job, and then Dusty and I will go with you."

"Okay." Kendra headed up the bank to the house.

CHAPTER 15

*I*t took until nightfall to recover Erica's body and turn it over to the medical examiner. After that Dusty drove Kendra to the house off Forest Lake Drive on the west end of Spencer. Joe followed in his official vehicle. Once inside, Kendra let Joe take the lead, because he'd done this sort of thing before. He was extremely kind to Lacey, telling her the facts as gently as he could.

"Do you have a friend I can call for you?" he asked.

Kendra waited for the reply.

"You could call Roy Barns for me," she finally answered. "He's a friend."

The name was familiar. Kendra remembered her mom knowing a guy named Roy a long time ago. Joe offered Lacey his sympathies and left.

"We'll stay with you until your friend comes," Dusty said.

Lacey offered them coffee, but Kendra went to make it. The kitchen was still old and outdated, but clean, if not tidy. The refrigerator held colorful crayon drawings with Ian's name scrawled at the top. She touched one and ran her fingertips over the waxy red splotches of color. Lacey kept these on display like a proud parent or grandparent. Her opinion of her moved ever so slightly on the disapproval scale.

She had forgiven her, after all.

She carried their mugs of coffee into the other room. "Did anyone want milk or sugar?"

"No thanks," Dusty and Lacey said at the same time.

"You were always the strong one," she said to Kendra. "You looked like a breeze would blow you over, but you were full of grit. Erica acted tough and she talked tough, and she had a mean streak, that girl did."

Dusty took Kendra's hand and Lacey noticed. "Are you two together again?"

"I hope so," Dusty answered. "I've loved your daughter since we were kids."

"Is it true, these charges that were brought against Erica?"

Dusty nodded. "It's true. The investigators had evidence on her phone and proof of her purchasing the ingredients to make the drugs."

She set down her mug with a hand that trembled. "I'm sorry."

"You didn't do it," he said. "You didn't know, did you?"

She shook her head. "I believed her."

"Kendra...?" Lacey looked up at her. She appeared weary, and the lines around her mouth and eyes were more pronounced. There was gray at her temples where her harshly-colored blond hair was growing out. She'd lived her life the way she wanted to, maybe the only way she knew how. She'd been a crappy parent, and they both knew it. "I'm sorry I wasn't the mother you deserved. You deserved better. I know that."

Kendra didn't feel the gratification she imagined. Her emotions were a letdown in one respect but told her something important in another. She was never nurtured by the one person who should have made her feel accepted and loved, but the gnawing sense of rejection she'd known her whole life was no longer threatening to swallow her. This woman had given birth to daughters in a situation where she wasn't equipped or capable of giving them guidance or perhaps of even recognizing their needs until it was too late.

Kendra had survived because she'd learned to parent herself through her aunt's influence and the Cavanaughs' example.

"I've already forgiven you," she said.

Lacey blinked in surprise. "You have?"

"And Erica as well. I'm done with bitterness."

Dusty looked over at her.

"I am," she reiterated. "I'm not angry. I'm sad and I'm disappointed, but I'm letting it go. I never wanted this to happen to Erica."

"She was a troubled young woman," Lacey agreed.

There was a knock at the door, and Dusty got up to let in a man in jeans and a button-down western shirt with pearl snaps. He had reddish gray hair and was balding on the top and wore a mustache.

"Roy, this is my daughter, Kendra and her...boyfriend, I guess, right? Dusty Cavanaugh. This here's Roy Barns."

Dusty shook his hand.

"Your brother's the sheriff," Roy said.

Dusty nodded.

Roy looked uncomfortable, but he took a seat beside Lacey on the sofa.

Lacey explained what had happened. "The sheriff, Joe, thought I needed someone here with me."

"What's going to happen now?" Roy asked.

"There's no longer a defendant," Dusty answered. "So, nothing more will happen."

"Dusty will still appeal the judge to seal those reports, so this will never come out," Kendra said.

"Ian won't know what Erica did?" Lacey asked.

Dusty shook his head. "No one will know. When he's older, if there's a time when he's ready to know the truth, we'll figure that out."

"That's good," Lacey said. "Thanks for coming. Roy will help me from here on."

"Do you want help with a funeral?" Kendra asked.

"That would be real nice," Lacey answered.

Kendra stood and reached for Dusty's hand. They left and he helped her into the passenger side of his truck.

"No one could have seen this coming," he said as he pulled out onto Forest Lake Drive. "I admire you."

"In a way Erica was right about a lot of things."

"Like what?"

"She didn't have someone like you. She didn't have your family in her corner for support."

He reached over and threaded his fingers with hers. "She might have, if she hadn't done what she did. She made some really bad decisions."

"I did too. I ran off, rather than listen to you or stick around and figure it out."

"Understandable."

"I thought I bought Aunt Sophie's house because it was my safe place and held good memories. I thought I came to Spencer every summer to get away from performing and teach. Those things are true, but I see now that they were only part of my motivation. I bought the house and I came to Spencer every summer because I knew you were here."

He looked at her but turned his attention back to the road.

"I avoided running into you, but I knew I'd see you eventually and have to face the past."

"I'm glad I'm not your past anymore."

"Could you come home with me tonight? Do you think your mom would mind? I'm sure Chloe is good without me."

"I'd love to come home with you."

When they reached her house, Kendra checked the kitchen, where everything had been cleaned up and put away while they'd been waiting for the lake patrol. Dusty lit her lantern and they checked the yard. There were a few small holes in the ground where the badminton net had been staked.

"All is well," he said.

"Look." She pointed.

In the moonlight, the mama wood duck waddled across her lawn where it sloped toward the lake, four ducklings scurrying behind her. From the bank, the female's mate called, and she answered. Night was closing in, and the little family was settling in for the night.

She took Dusty's hand, and they walked down to where the water lapped against the shore. In the distance on the far side, the lights in the Aspen Gold Lodge's marina twinkled. From somewhere faint music drifted on the night breeze. "It's like nothing ever happened."

He squeezed her hand.

"What happened today will not change how I feel about this place or about the lake. Our private place was always over there somewhere." She pointed to the dense foliage to the north. "We made a lot of memories there. Even as recent as that dance in the dark."

He raised her hand to his lips and kissed the backs of her fingers.

"But we will make good memories here too. I'll keep this house and land forever."

"Of course."

"Someday our kids will spend summers here with their kids and hear the wood ducks."

Her words burst into Dusty's consciousness and sent a tingle of anticipation up his spine. "Our kids?"

"Ian and all the other beautiful kids we're going to have."

"Redheads," he said with a smile as wide as Colorado.

"I want to ask you something."

"Anything."

She turned to face him and took both of his hands in hers. If she wanted him to move to Denver, he'd make it work somehow. His heart beat a little raggedly.

"Dusty Cavanaugh, will you marry me?"

Good thing he hadn't locked his knees, because that was the last thing he'd expected, though the most welcome question he could imagine. She hadn't even needed to ask. "Yes."

She released his hands, reached behind her neck and came away with a chain. Moonlight glimmered from a ring dangling in the center, and even in this dim light he knew it was her engagement ring. She removed it from the chain, put the chain in her pocket and the ring in his left palm.

The silver was warm from her body. He reached for it, and she held out her hand. Dusty slipped the ring on her finger. His throat threatened to close on him, but he managed to say in a hoarse whisper, *"Forever dancing to the beat of our hearts."*

The inscription inside the ring. The ring that had spent years at the bottom of Twin Owl Lake and had then been amazingly recovered by an old fisherman just in time for this day. Dusty didn't claim to understand fate, but the unexplainable events that had led to placing this very ring on her finger made him a believer. "I think we should name our next son Jonas."

"I think that would be appropriate," she agreed.

He kissed her then to seal the promise.

❦

Three weeks later

Add the convenience of the groom's sister being the event planner at the Aspen Gold Lodge to the fact that Jakob Spencer was his great uncle made for a grand wedding reception. Steph had miraculously put the whole thing together in a ridiculously short amount of time.

The east lawn at Aspen Gold Lodge looked like something out of a movie set with an enormous tulle-draped canopy for the food, tables and chairs, and another with a parquet floor and strands of fairy lights for dancing. Steph told her this floor had only been used on rare occasions, and apparently their wedding qualified as one of those, because here they were, she in an off-the-shoulder white satin gown and Dusty in a fitted tux.

Dusty and Kendra had said their I dos under honest-to-goodness crystal chandeliers and before an arched window that had been suspended from the steel beams of the canopy to frame the stunning mountain vista. Photographers had taken a hundred photos, and family and friends gathered to congratulate them. After enjoying a delicious catered meal, an orchestra played pop tunes, and dozens of people filled the dance floor.

"Did everyone from Spencer show up for this?" Kendra asked Dusty.

"Not everyone."

"Oh, because there are a few people you're not related to, right?"

He grinned. "Friends, of course."

"Of course."

Kendra had invited only a half a dozen colleagues who

had flown in and were staying at the lodge. "My friends take up one table."

"Not anymore."

Zoe Barlow approached them. "Congratulations and best wishes," she said. "You two make a beautiful couple."

"Thank you." Kendra gave her a bright smile.

Dusty gave the woman a hug. "Zoe and I are second cousins. Zoe and my dad were first cousins."

"I adored your dad," Zoe said. "One of the most genuinely kind men I ever knew."

"We've run into each other on Friday nights," Kendra said to him about Zoe. "You're Jakob's oldest daughter, right?"

"I prefer *first* daughter," she answered with a grin. Her floral summer dress showed off a slim, athletic figure. Only a few gray strands showed in her shoulder-length golden-brown hair.

A short woman with spiky dark-blond hair joined them. Zoe greeted her. "Kendra, do you know Muffy Burnham?"

"I don't think so. Hello, Muffy. Is it Burnham, like the hospital?"

"Yes. Edna Burnham was my great-grandmother. My grandmother named the hospital after her."

"Burnham was my mother's maiden name," Zoe explained.

Kendra held up a hand. "Nope, I don't even want to attempt to figure out how you two are related."

Zoe flattened her palm against Kendra's. "Now that you're a Cavanaugh, just you wait fifty years—someone will be saying that to your kids and grandkids."

Kendra rolled her eyes. "You're right."

The orchestra swept into an instrumental version of *Perfect* just then. She turned and looked up at her new husband.

"I requested this song for us." He took her hand. Smiling guests parted for them to make their way to the dancefloor.

He sang softly against her hair, *"I found a love...for me...."*

"Could you be any more perfect yourself, Dusty Cavanaugh?"

"Don't puff me up into something I'm not. I'm just a guy... dancing with a girl."

She laughed aloud. He made her deliriously happy. He was funny, romantic, kind, and he even knew her favorite songs and foods and movies.

"They'll be playing this every half hour, so that way I can't lose you for long. Find me each time."

"Did you pay extra for that?"

"Yeah. Pricier than slipping Loydell a roll of quarters."

"Is that what you did at the VFW that night?"

"Maybe. And I wanted you to get more use out of Grandma's dancing slippers."

Kendra pulled aside the hem of her skirt, so he could see the satin embroidered slippers Naomi had given her.

He smiled and met her eyes.

Another couple maneuvered close to them. Crosby was dashing in dark trousers and a cream-colored summer jacket. Kendra didn't recognize his short dark-haired plus one. He introduced her as Gemma.

"It's a pleasure to meet you," Gemma," Kendra told her. They changed partners for the next song, and she told Crosby softly, "I hope you know Brianna and I are staying friends."

"I'm cool with that. I'm staying friends with her too."

Jonas cut in, delighting Kendra. He wore a three-piece suit, a shirt and tie, and had gotten a haircut and his white beard trimmed.

"You are quite the dashing gentleman this evening, Mr. Finch."

He grinned. "Couldn't miss you two lovebirds tyin' the knot. I feel like I had somethin' to do with gettin' you together."

"I've remembered what you told me about Rebecca. That she was your one and only. That's how it is with Dusty and me. He's the only one for me."

"I knew that the minute you looked at that ring, and I saw your face."

She held her hand open between them, to show him the ring on her finger snugly nestled beside a wedding band. "We had to get married after you went to all the trouble of bringing my ring up from the bottom of the lake."

"So you did. And your mama's here. Piper showed me which one she is."

Kendra had spoken to Jonas only a week or so ago, and he knew what had happened to Erica. She don't look like the devil reincarnated."

"Is that what Piper told you? She's a little protective of me." She spotted Lacey sitting with Ian and Roy Barns at one of the tables that had been moved over and set up just inside the perimeter of the tent. Kendra had taken her to have her hair colored and styled, and she almost blended in with the rest of the guests. "We're never going to have a close relationship. Too much has happened for that, but I've forgiven her for her inability to be a good parent. She's really trying to be a good grandparent to Ian. He loves her, and that's what's important."

Erica's death had been senseless, but nothing Kendra could ever have done would have made a difference. Her sister had made poor decisions her whole life, perhaps searching for what was missing or trying to numb the pain of rejection. Those decisions had led her down a path of destruction. Kendra was in the process of shutting the door on that chapter of her life and embracing her future.

"Dusty and I plan to name our next son after you,"

"Jonas ain't my first name," he revealed with a sly grin. "Are you sure you want a son named Fitzgerald?"

She looked at him wide-eyed. "Good to know. We're sticking with Jonas."

He cackled.

The music changed, and as Dusty had predicted the orchestra again played the music he'd requested.

"Excuse me. I have to find my husband for this song."

"Forever dancin' to the beat of your hearts?" Jonas asked. He'd seen the inscription inside her ring.

She nodded, gave him a hug and took her leave.

Dusty was waiting for her several feet away, a smile on his lips and a promise in his eyes. His was still the face she wanted to see every day, his the expression she wanted to watch as he spotted her across a room.

"I'm the proudest man in the world tonight." He rested his hand on the small of her back and led her among the other dancers.

"And I'm the luckiest woman."

His kiss tasted like wine and hinted of the years ahead.

"'Darlin', you look perfect tonight....'"

Dear Reader,

Once upon a time a group of writer friends—helping a member with a particularly difficult thread in a continuity series contrived by her editors—got the grandiose idea to create a continuity series of their own.

Yes, this was us, and we threw ourselves wholeheartedly into developing characters, fashioning families, family dynamics, and a setting, which evolved from one member's love of all things Colorado. We created family trees, character profiles, detailed maps, brainstormed titles and themes. We collected photos and researched and even started the stories. We proposed our idea to a few publishers and got no traction. So, after a time the contracted books came first, two members dropped out of the group, a couple new ones came and went. But the core group remained.

In a tragic turn of events we lost a beloved friend and co-writer. Grief took the remaining wind from our sails. We recovered slowly, welcomed a new friend to our critique group. Then came a day when we got together and said, "We're going to get serious and do this!" Energy built, and the series took on new life. A previous co-creator joined us again. Now, here we are, years after the initial idea, sharing the finished stories with you and hoping you will feel the same intensity and appreciation for this project as we do. We have many more stories to share, and the ideas keep coming. Look for more books to follow in Aspen Gold: The Series.

So, come along. We welcome you to Spencer, Colorado, to have a look inside the families, to laugh in their good times and cry in their sad times, to follow them as they solve mysteries, expose secrets, recover from their pasts, reach for their goals, and most importantly—as they fall in love.

ASPEN GOLD SERIES

The Aspen Gold Books
   Dancing In The Dark Cheryl St.John
   He had everything a man could want--except her forgiveness...
   Call Me Mandy Debra Hines
   The last man Miranda loved took everything from her...
   Ryder's Heart *lizzie starr
   Ryder discovers an intriguing woman in his bed...
   For Keeps Barbara Gwen & *lizzie starr
   Hiding the truth is like denying the sun...
   Second Chances Donna Kaye
   She tried the fairy tale and the fairy tale didn't work...
   Sleepin' Alone Bernadette Jones
   Hunter Lawe...riding the line between enforcing the law and
breaking it...

Also *Coming soon* a new tale from M.A. Jewell

To learn more about the Aspen Gold Series, the books and authors, visit our website and sign up for the Rocky Mountain Rumors newsletter!

We love to hear from our readers. Contact the Aspen Gold authors at mailto:rumors@aspengoldseries.com

ABOUT THE AUTHOR

Cheryl has always loved the exciting and diverse worlds available between the covers of books. As a child she wrote stories & drew covers, then stapled them into little books. She cut all the tiny images from the book club advertisements in the Sunday newspaper & glued them to bits of cardboard so Barbie® had a full library.

Cheryl is the married author of more than fifty books, both historical and contemporary. Her stories have earned numerous RITA nominations, Romantic Times awards & are published in over a dozen languages. One thing all reviewers & readers agree on regarding Cheryl's work is the degree of emotion & believability. In describing her stories of second chances & redemption, readers & reviewers use words like, "emotional punch, hometown feel, core values, believable characters & real-life situations." Amazon & Goodreads reviews show her popularity with readers.

The author lives in the Midwest, USA. When she's not writing or spending time with her family, she's checking out garage sales, flea markets & antique malls. Among her collections are teacups & teapots, roosters, chicken kitchen timers, vintage spice tins, wooden recipe boxes, Barbies®, charm bracelets, vintage jewelry, Kokeshi dolls, white stoneware, Delftware, souvenir spoons, Goebel birds, Royal Copley planters, vintage hankies & BOOKS. Cheryl admits she's a bargain hunter with the heart of a hoarder, trying to live as a minimalist. The struggle is real.

Check out Cheryl's amazon author page to see an entire listing of all of her books.

facebook.com/CherylStJ

twitter.com/_CherylStJohn_

instagram.com/cherylstjohn

pinterest.com/cheryl_stjohn

bookbub.com/profile/cheryl-st-john

SAINT OR SINNER

SAINT OR SINNER
American Western Historical

In this heartwarming tale of redemption, Joshua McBride

returns from the war a changed man, ready to put down roots and plant his feet in the community. Prim and uptight Miss Adelaide Stapleton, leader of the Dorcas Society, doesn't believe he's changed—people are never what they seem. But she has plenty of secrets of her own—among them the inescapable fact that Joshua sets her heart to pounding and makes her long for his disturbing kisses. How long can she keep her own past hidden—and resist temptation?

LAND OF DREAMS
American Western Historical

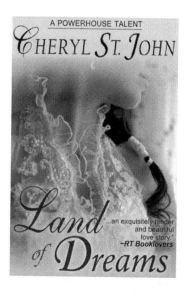

In this tale of hope and love, too-tall spinster Thea Coulson wants to be a mother to a child who arrives in Nebraska on an orphan train. When Booker Hayes shows up to take his niece, a marriage of convenience suits them both. Thea's nights are filled with dreams of the tall, dark army major, but she guards her heart. Booker's first taste of home and hearth has him longing for more, but first he must win the trust of his niece...and the heart of the sun-kissed farmer's daughter.

RAIN SHADOW

Dutch Country Brides Book 2
American Western Historical

Raised by the Lakota Sioux and having traveled with the Wild West Show for many years, Rain Shadow is unprepared for a forced stay at the home of Anton Neubauer while her son recuperates. He is a rock, a man who has lived on and farmed the same several hundred acres since he was young.

Anton needs a mother for his son, but he needs someone domestic and ladylike, not the Smith & Wesson toting female who sets up her teepee in his front yard and whose target practice wakes him at the crack of dawn. But fate, two little boys and two old men conspire to keep them together, and it's too late to deny their passion once love is part of the equation.

JOE'S WIFE
American Western Historical

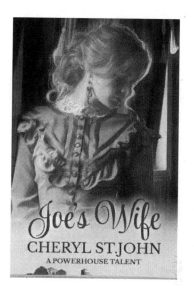

After Meg Telford's husband dies in the war and is lauded as a hero, she can't keep the ranch without a man to shoulder the workload. Nothing will stop her from saving Joe's dream. The war has taken nearly all the able-bodied men—and a devilishly handsome bad boy seems her only choice.

Town pariah, Tye Hatcher has a reputation as a hell-raiser, but he's looking to prove himself and has his own plans for her land. Meg's proposal might be too good to be true, but he's willing to take a chance, even if the risk is his heart.

Struggling with the rejection of the townspeople and guilt over her changing feelings for this convenient new husband, Meg's vulnerable dreams and their hard work will be for naught unless she and Tye reveal their secrets. Neither can change the past, but is a better future within their grasp?

A HUSBAND BY ANY OTHER NAME
Contemporary Romance

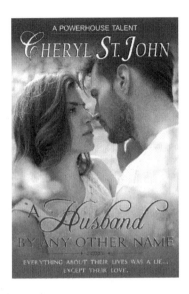

Fourteen years ago Dan Beckett's identical twin took off without a word to his pregnant young fiancé or their father. Having secretly loved Lorraine for years, Dan assumes his twin's identity as Lorraine's husband and father of the baby she carried. Around the lie, he created the perfect life.

Now his greatest fear is coming true. His long-lost brother is coming home—with amnesia. Dan is about to lose his tenuous hold on this masquerade.

Lorrie built a life with Tom Beckett, the man she loves, the father of her children—but her whole married life has been a lie. Will the truth unravel the love they once shared? What will become of their family, their children...their marriage when everyone learns the truth?

After years of being asked for recipes, Cheryl St.John spent a summer writing down ingredients and baking times, baking and asking for beta testers in order to put together this collection of mouthwatering recipes for Bundt cakes. Many of the recipes are labeled NO SKILL REQUIRED, indicating exceptional ease of preparation. If you don't consider yourself a baker or if you're an accomplished baker and simply want a quick recipe, you will find the cakes using box mixes are convenient and delicious. You don't have to tell anyone you started with a mix—the cakes are so good that no one will guess preparation didn't take hours. Bake with ease and enjoy serving a beautiful cake to family and friends.

Cheryl's philosophy: Eat cake!
It's someone's birthday somewhere.

Made in the
USA
Lexington, KY